P9-CRT-076

"Daybreak" written by Nancy Lambert.
Illustrated by Mirco Pierfederici and Chris Sotomayor.
Based on the Marvel comic book series *The Avengers*.

"Small Hero, Big Thrills!" written by Andy Schmidt.
Illustrated by Ron Lim and Rachelle Rosenberg.
Based on the Marvel comic book series *The Avengers*.

"No *I* in *Team*" written by Nancy Lambert.
Illustrated by Andrea Di Vito, Rachelle Rosenberg, and Peter Pantazis.
Based on the Marvel comic book series *The Avengers*.

"Practice Makes Perfect" written by Arie Kaplan.
Illustrated by Andrea Di Vito and Rachelle Rosenberg.
Based on the Marvel comic book series *The Avengers*.

"Dino Time" written by Colin Hosten.
Illustrated by Khoi Pham and Paul Mounts.
Based on the Marvel comic book series *The Avengers*.

"Not Easy Being Big and Green" written by Cristina Garces.
Illustrated by Ron Lim and Rachelle Rosenberg.
Based on the Marvel comic book series *The Avengers*.

"Lending a Wing" written by Arie Kaplan.
Illustrated by Ron Lim and Rachelle Rosenberg.
Based on the Marvel comic book series *The Avengers*.

"Calling All Avengers!" written by Andy Schmidt.
Illustrated by Andrea Di Vito and Rachelle Rosenberg.
Based on the Marvel comic book series *The Avengers*.

"Freaky Thor Day" written by Nancy Lambert.
Illustrated by Mirco Pierfederici and Chris Sotomayor.
Based on the Marvel comic book series *The Avengers*.

"Robin Hawk" written by Arie Kaplan.
Illustrated by Mirco Pierfederici and Chris Sotomayor.
Based on the Marvel comic book series *The Avengers*.

"Friends for Life" written by Andy Schmidt.
Illustrated by Mirco Pierfederici and Chris Sotomayor.
Based on the Marvel comic book series *The Avengers*.

"The Rise of a New Team" written by Clarissa Wong.
Illustrated by Andrea Di Vito and Rachelle Rosenberg.
Based on the Marvel comic book series *The Avengers*.

marvelkids.com
© 2015 MARVEL

All rights reserved. Published by Marvel Press, an imprint of Disney Book Group. No part of this book
may be reproduced or transmitted in any form or by any means, electronic or mechanical, including
photocopying, recording, or by information storage and retrieval system, without written permission from
the publisher. For information address Marvel Press, 125 West End Avenue, New York, New York 10023.

Printed in the United States of America

First Edition, November 2015

3 5 7 9 10 8 6 4 2

FAC-038091-18120

ISBN 978-1-4847-4331-7

Library of Congress Control Number: 2015901551

SUSTAINABLE
FORESTRY
INITIATIVE

Certified Sourcing
www.sfiprogram.org
SFI-00993

This Label Applies to Text Stock Only

CONTENTS

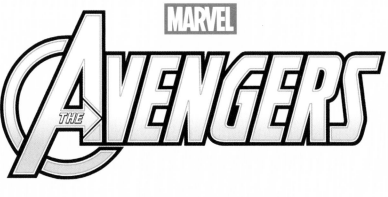

Daybreak

One morning, while Captain America, Black Widow, and Hawkeye were training on the beach, they saw something frightening. A bright beam of light pierced the sky and almost split it in two! Then, as suddenly as it had appeared, it vanished. The Avengers stopped in their tracks.

"Whoa—what was that?" asked Hawkeye.

"Lightning?" Captain America suggested.

"But there isn't a cloud in the sky, and Thor is back at Avengers Tower," said Black Widow.

"I'd better go check it out. It's probably nothing," Cap said, "but you two should head back to the Helicarrier and fill in Fury."

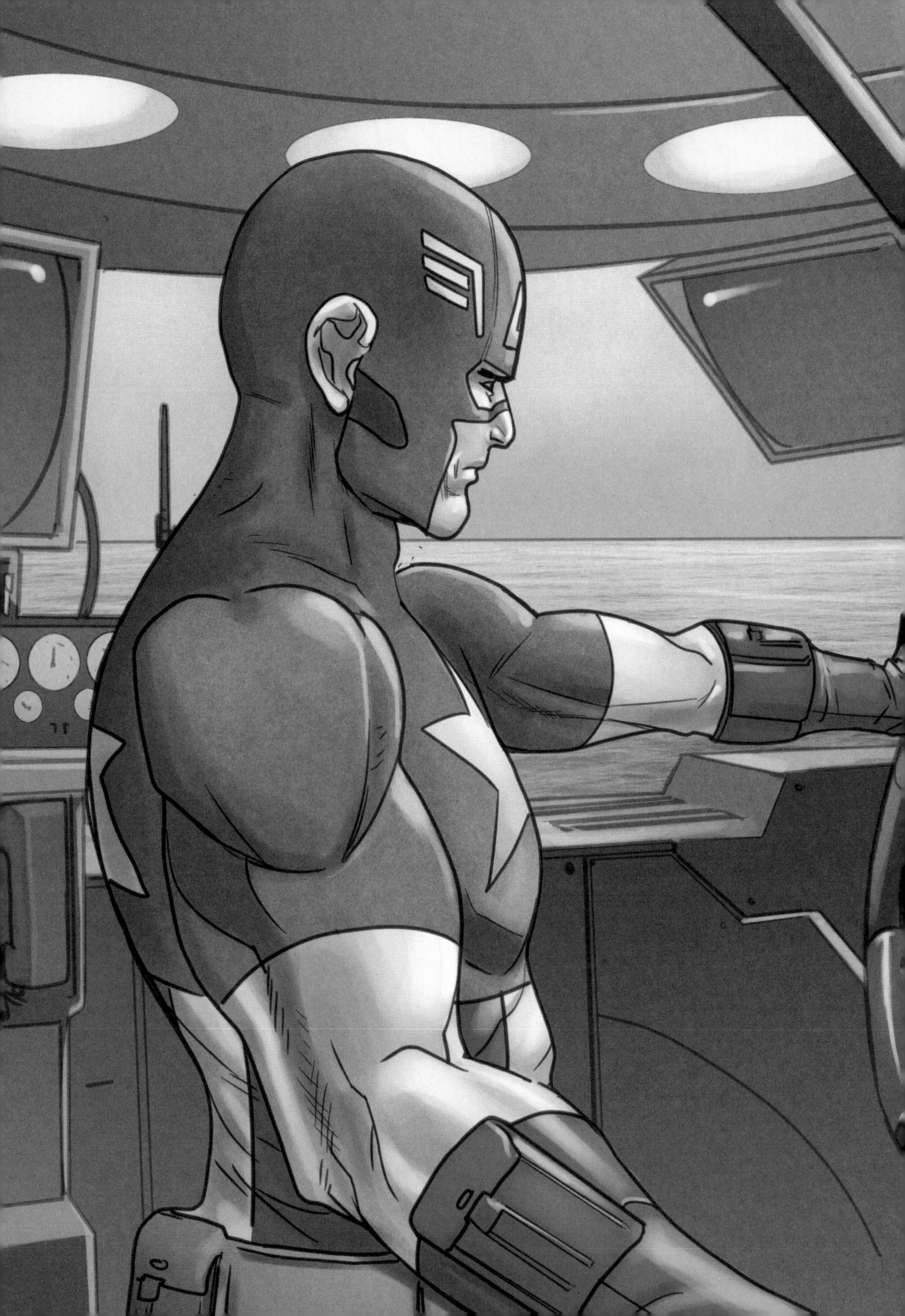

Moments later, Captain America took one of the S.H.I.E.L.D. harbor-patrol units out to sea. Nick Fury directed him from a screen in the dashboard.

"You should see the island by now, Cap," he said.

"I don't see anything. Just a lot of debris."

"According to this map," Fury said, "you shouldn't even be in the water anymore. You should be on land."

Suddenly, the communication screen flickered and hissed. Cap could no longer see or talk to Nick Fury. The screen went dark for a moment, and then Red Skull's face appeared.

"Beautiful day isn't it, Captain?" he said, laughing.

"Schmidt," Captain America growled. "What have you done, Schmidt?"

"Just sent a little message . . . or a dozen." The screen began flashing with video clips that showed other landmarks, mountains, and monuments disintegrating seconds after being hit with a blinding light similar to the one the Avengers had seen that morning.

"But how? Another Infinity Gem?" Cap asked.

"No. I've harnessed a new force unlike that of the gods." Red Skull smirked.

"Then what's the point of this senseless destruction?" Cap asked.

"Oh, just the sworn allegiance of every world leader by sunrise tomorrow," Red Skull replied. "Anyone who does not comply will find they no longer have a country to lead."

The screen flickered again and went black.

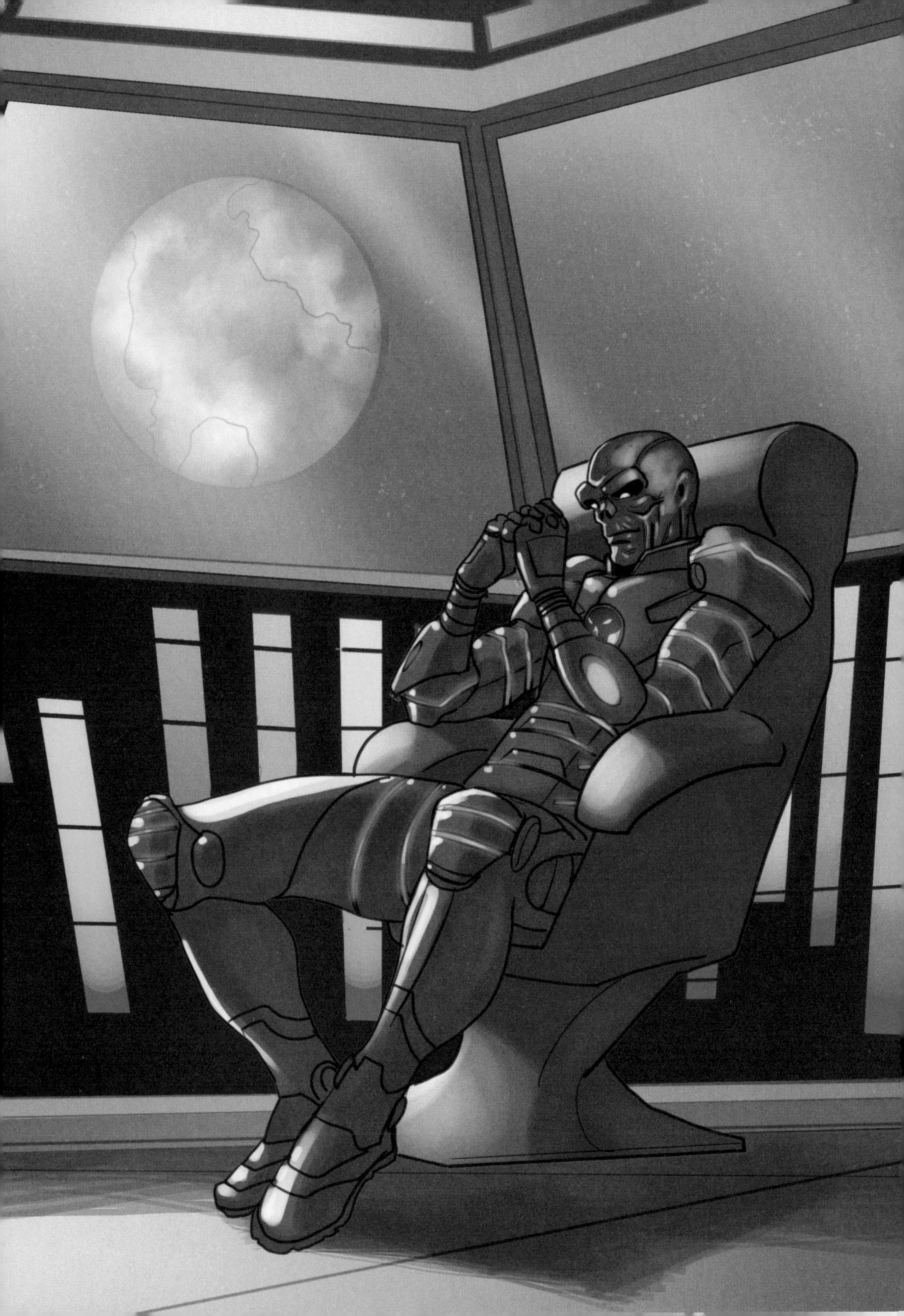

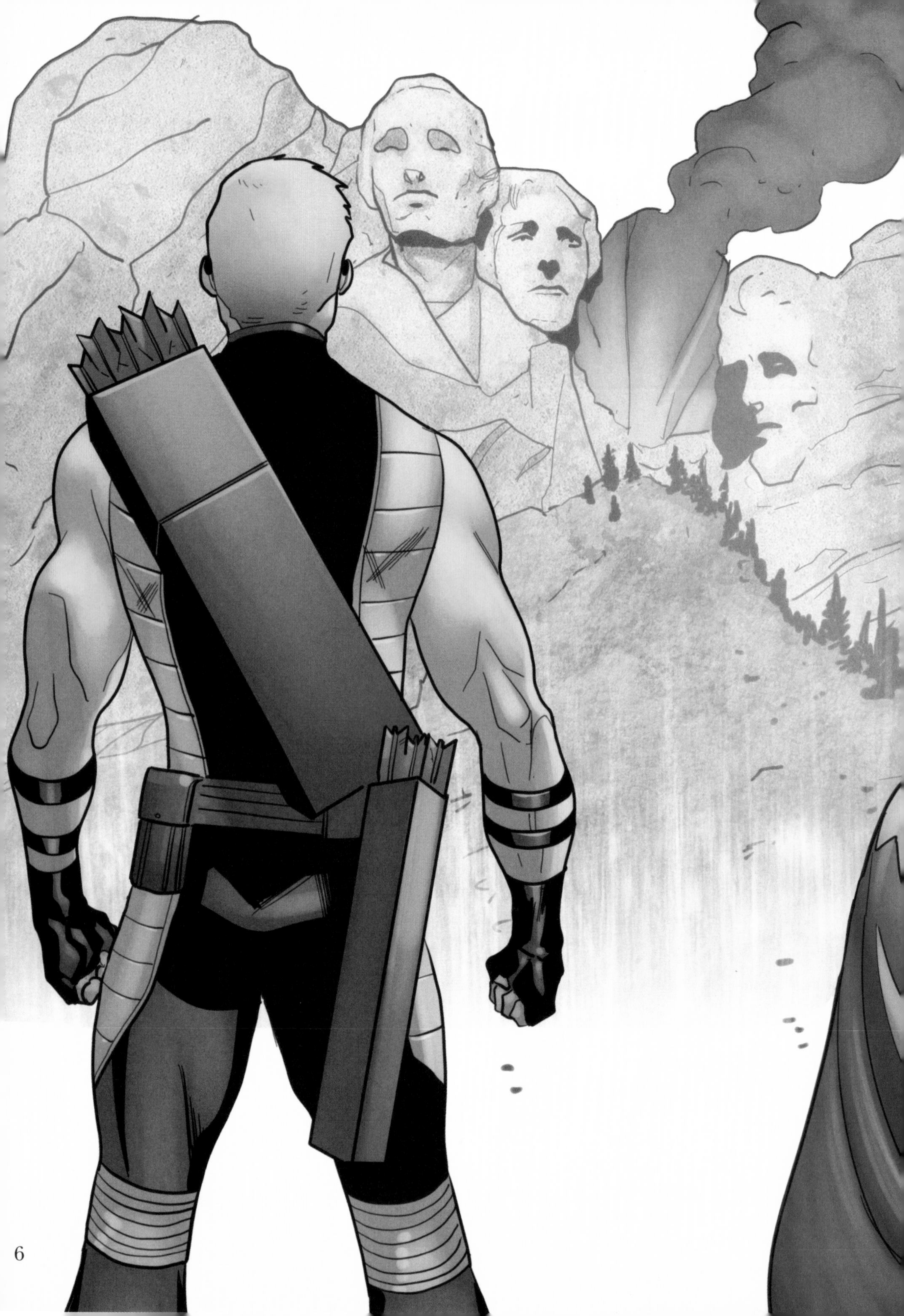

Captain America couldn't believe Red Skull's claims were true. He called Fury.

"Do we have confirmation that any of those images are real?"

"I've sent Avengers to do recon on some of the sites," Fury said. "But I still need someone to check the others. Will you do it, Cap?"

"Just tell me where to begin," said Captain America.

It was the same at every site the Avengers visited that day. They only believed it because they had seen it with their own eyes. Hawkeye was at Mount Rushmore, and he noticed one of the faces in the mountain was missing. In Egypt, Black Widow found that some ancient landmarks had been scrubbed away, as if erased from time. Luckily, so far, all Red Skull's targets had been uninhabited. But Cap shuddered when he thought about Red Skull making good on his threat at dawn.

"I won't give him the chance,"

Cap vowed.

Back at S.H.I.E.L.D. headquarters, Fury slammed his hand on the console in frustration.

"Where could a device powerful enough to wipe out entire mountain ranges be hiding?" Fury asked.

"And somehow also be able to reach every corner of the Earth?" Cap added. He tapped the touchscreen and pulled up a map. "These are all the known blast sites. They're scattered across the globe. How could he move a weapon like that without someone noticing?"

Then Cap and Fury stared at the map silently for a moment. Cap snapped his fingers. "He's not moving it."

Cap tapped some coordinates into the computer. The screen pulled up satellite images of space, then zoomed in on the sun. Cap touched the screen again, and the camera revealed the silhouette of a hulking metallic space station against the furious amber glow of the sun's surface.

"He must be using something on this station to focus the thermonuclear energy of the sun and turn it into a powerful weapon," Cap explained.

Fury drummed his fingers on the screen. "Well, if we can't take out the sun . . ."

"Then we take out his device," finished Cap.

"The sun's ninety-two million miles away. Sunrise is in a few hours. We need to get to the spot of the first sunrise. But it's a risky move—we may not make it there in time."

Cap took a deep breath. "I can go. I might need Tony Stark for a few quick modifications first, though."

High atop Mount Hikurangi in New Zealand, where the sun first hits the Earth every day, Captain America watched the countdown clock on his wrist communicator tick away the minutes till dawn.

"Are you sure you want to do this alone, Cap?" Fury's voice came over the headset.

"We only have one chance to get this right," Captain America said. "If it doesn't work, it's better that the rest of the Avengers be on hand to respond."

At that moment, Red Skull's face appeared on television, computer, and phone screens across the planet.

"I understand that you have failed to meet my demands."

"We'll never submit to you," Cap said.

"Then you'll pay the ultimate price."

Red Skull's transmission cut off.

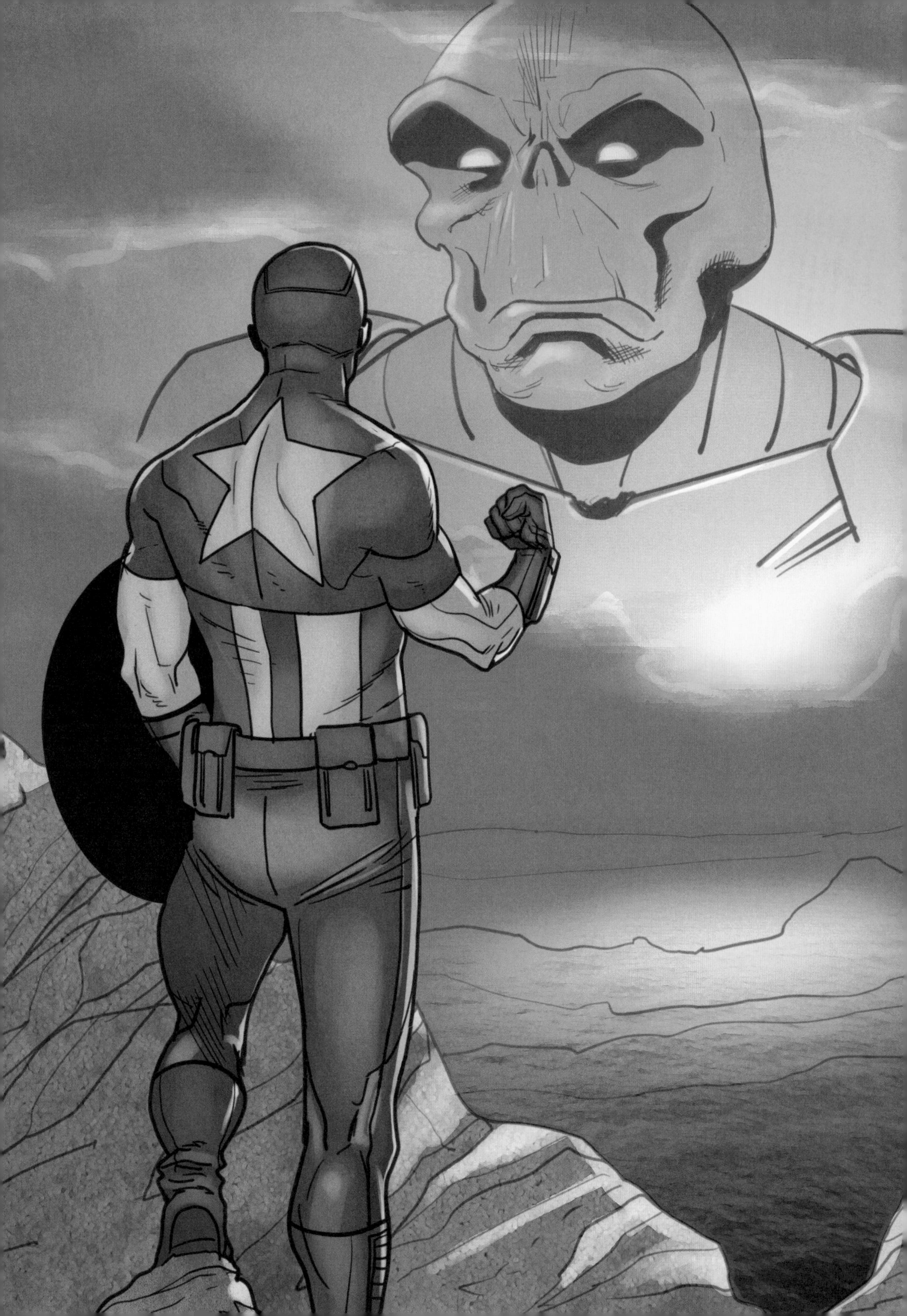

A sharp beam of white light cut through the sky, racing toward Captain America. Cap angled his shield toward the incoming ray. When it hit the shield, the air around Captain America seemed to explode. He grunted as he fought against the force of the beam, its energy relentlessly cascading off the shield's rounded surface.

Cap heard Red Skull's mocking voice over his headset.

"Captain Rogers, even a creation as remarkable as you has limits. You can't be everywhere at once, and I can recalibrate my laser to hit any part of the Earth at any time," he hissed. "Let me demonstrate."

The beam cut off suddenly and then reappeared a few yards away, slicing into the earth near Cap's feet. Black smoke rose through the air as the ground was obliterated. The mountain began to collapse into the void.

But Cap knew what to do. He flipped his shield so the inside, with Iron Man's updates, faced out like a reflective lens, and then he leapt beneath the beam one more time. Cap took a few staggering steps back. His hands shook with the effort of holding the shield steady, angling it just so. The shield grew red-hot, then white-hot, but it did not yield—and neither did Cap. Suddenly, the beam itself seemed to grow brighter. It reversed direction, reflecting off the shield and shooting back into the sky—and then it abruptly disappeared.

Cap took a shaky breath and braced himself for another attack. But it didn't come.

He heard Fury's voice over his headset.

"You did it, Cap! Satellite images confirm you destroyed the magnifier!"

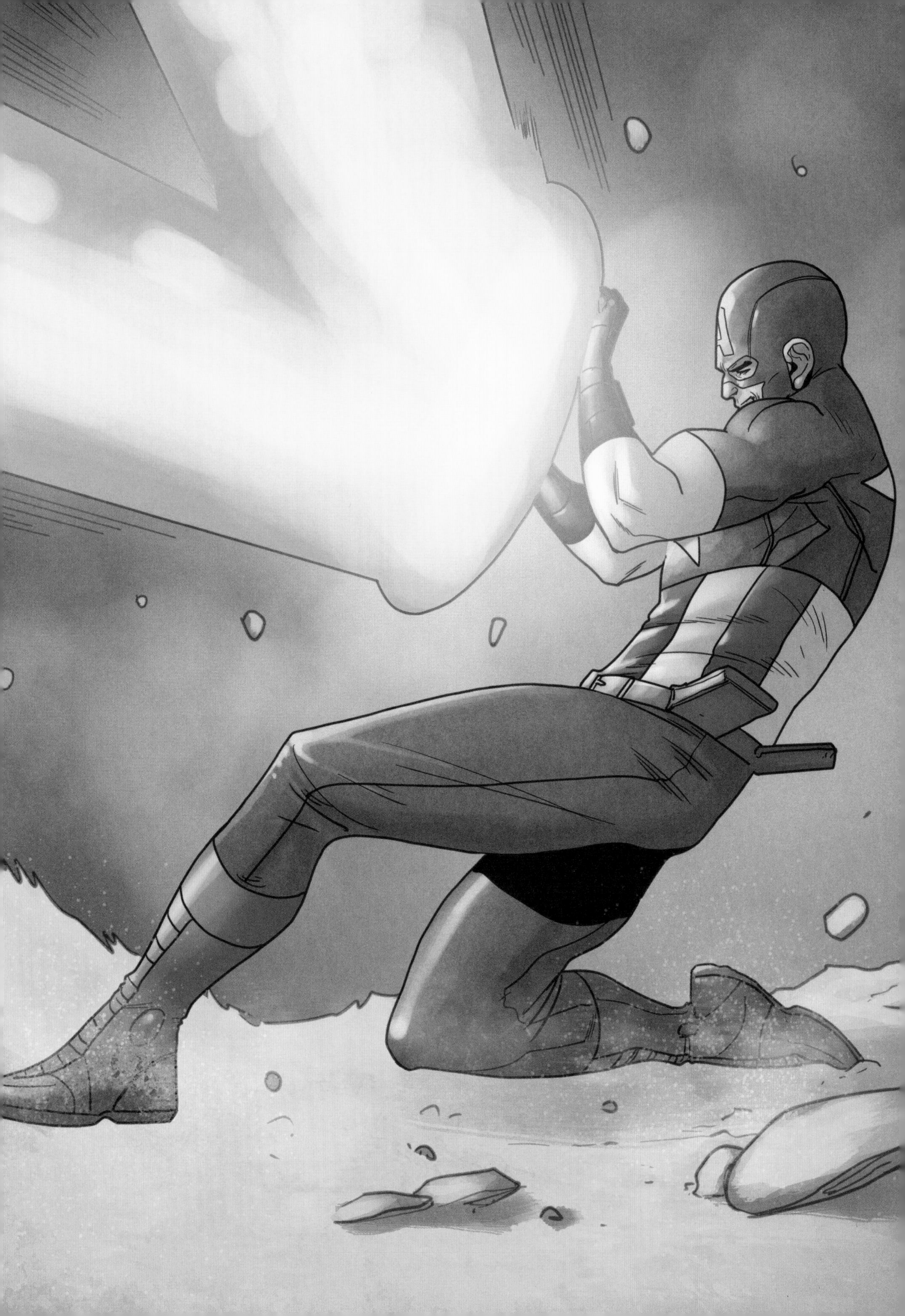

Later, when Cap returned to the S.H.I.E.L.D. Helicarrier, he had one burning question for Fury.

"Any sign of Red Skull?" Cap asked.

"We've sent a wreckage unit to search, but so far there's no sign of him."

Captain America nodded. "At least we destroyed that thing."

"Yes," Fury said. Then he chuckled. "You're like a whole new level of sunblock—SPF Cap."

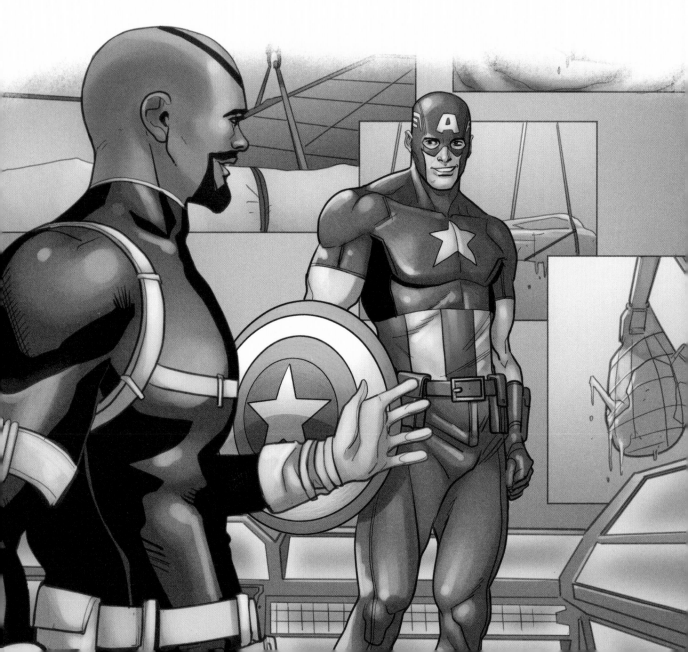

Small Hero, Big Thrills!

You've heard of Captain America and Iron Man, but do you know about Ant-Man? You may have missed him—he's only a few inches tall! But just because he's small doesn't mean he isn't a big hero.

One night, when Scott Lang was walking home with a teddy bear for his daughter, Cassie, two police cars sped by him with their sirens blaring. He was close to home and not too happy to see that some sort of crisis was happening near where he and his daughter lived.

When he looked where the police were heading, he saw that a band of the Avengers' fiercest foes was loose again. A normal person would have done the sensible thing: run for cover!

But Scott Lang had a secret.

He was not just a good guy with a young daughter. When he put on his costume, he became . . . Ant-Man!

Ant-Man was no fool, though! He knew he should call for help rather than take on all the foes by himself.

He pulled out his phone and called Avengers Tower to report the attack. The Avengers were on their way. *Whew,* Ant-Man thought. But just as he started to relax, the Super Villains were on the move!

I can't just let them go, he thought. *I've got to do something, even if the Avengers aren't here yet.*

When Scott thought about Cassie being so close, he got angry! *No,* he thought. *I won't allow these bullies to get away.*

Knowing the Avengers would be there soon, Ant-Man jumped into action. All he had to do was slow down the villains until the Avengers arrived, and then the Super Heroes would help. Ant-Man started with Batroc—a martial-arts expert sporting a tacky gold-and-purple suit. Even Super Villains should dress sharp!

After Batroc, Ant-Man took aim at the biggest villain of the bunch—a giant head with tiny arms and legs, called M.O.D.O.K.! This time, he called out to his flying insect friends and mounted a full assault right at M.O.D.O.K.'s eye.

Nothing can beat the swarm!

And just as the other foes were going to turn on Ant-Man . . .

. . . some of the Avengers arrived!

    With the Avengers' help, none of the sinister villains would go free. Ant-Man may not have been as strong as Hulk, or have flown as fast as Thor, or even have had all the cool gadgets that Iron Man did, but he sure was useful as they and some of the other Avengers tracked down the rest of the villains.

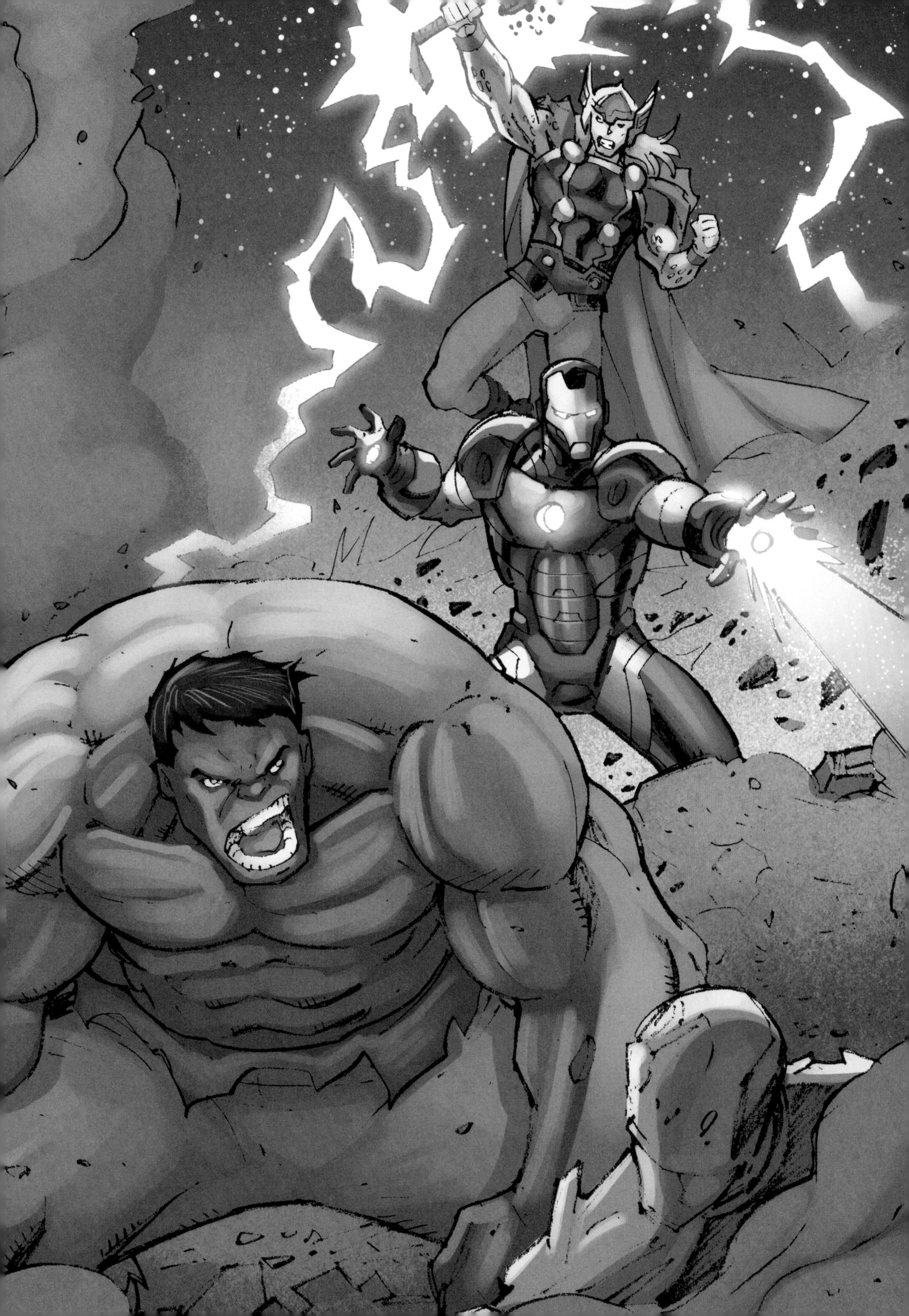

While the Avengers were going after the other bad guys,
Ant-Man, surprisingly, was best suited to take on Ultron by
himself! The other Avengers couldn't crack Ultron's sturdy
armor, but the tiniest hero didn't even have to try.

He simply sent his flying ants into Ultron's mouth and asked
them to start pulling on every wire they could find inside. Ultron
never stood a chance.

Hawkeye found Baron Von Strucker and Arnim Zola in a nearby warehouse. "Hey, Ant-Man!" Hawkeye called. "I've got an idea. You want to help?"

"You bet, Hawkeye!"

As Hawkeye fired his arrow at the two villains, neither of them suspected that another Super Hero was sitting on the end of it! "In your face, evildoers!" Ant-Man shouted. They never knew what—or who— hit them.

Black Widow tracked A.I.M. agents to a lab, but the door was locked. She asked Ant-Man for assistance. Together, they were able to get inside the lab quickly and quietly and spring a big surprise on the would-be world conquerors!

"Great work, Ant-Man," Black Widow said.

Much to Iron Man's surprise, the Crimson Dynamo had upgraded his armor.

Even Iron Man—*the* Iron Man—needed a little help from Ant-Man. Talk about leveling up!

As the day came to an end, Ant-Man had become friends with the Avengers. He had helped them defeat many of their foes. Iron Man asked whether Ant-Man wanted to go with them to fight other villains but was surprised when Ant-Man said, "Thanks a lot, Iron Man, but I'm going to pass on this one."

Iron Man asked, "Why is that? You have bigger villains to catch?" Ant-Man laughed at Iron Man's friendly question.

As totally awesome as it was to help the Avengers save the city—and it *was* awesome—Ant-Man had something more important to do than play hero.

"It must be pretty important," said Captain America.

"Not 'it,' Cap," said Ant-Man. "'She'! My daughter is at home waiting for me . . .

". . . and I've got a teddy bear to deliver!"

With his costume put away, Scott Lang was just Scott Lang again. Being a Super Hero was important, but being a great dad was even more important.

Cassie was thrilled to see her dad when he arrived and even happier to see her new teddy bear. She gave her dad the biggest hug ever. *Now I feel like a hero*, thought Scott.

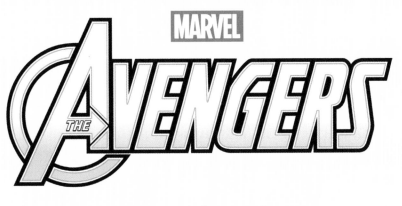
No *I* in *Team*

Clint Barton and Natasha Romanoff—better known to the world as Hawkeye and Black Widow—practiced together every morning. One day they decided to train in the park. The two old friends playfully ran through their exercises, trying to outdo each other.

"Natasha, wanna make training a little more interesting today?" Hawkeye asked.

"What do you mean?" said Black Widow.

"I bet you a big breakfast that I can hit that target from a hundred yards."

"Please," Natasha snorted. "You could do that in your sleep. Do it with more than one arrow and maybe I'll be impressed."

"Okay, how about three . . . at once?" said Clint.

Black Widow grinned. "This I have to see." She rubbed her stomach. "I can't wait for breakfast."

Hawkeye loaded three arrows into his bow. He pulled back on the bowstring, then shot all three toward the target at once. Each arrow hit the bull's-eye!

"Think you can top that, Natasha?" He smirked.

"I can do it with my eyes shut." Black Widow closed her eyes and shot two bolts from her Widow's Bite gauntlets. Both shots hit the target in the tiny space between Hawkeye's three arrows.

"Well, okay then," Hawkeye said with a laugh. "I guess hitting targets is one thing, but who do you think is better at stopping actual bad guys?"

"Me. Definitely," Natasha said.

"I'm not so sure."

Natasha smiled. "You think you're the best?"

"Let's find out. Why don't we split up today and see who can stop the most bad guys?"

"You're on. What do I win?" Black Widow asked.

"*If* you win, you mean," Hawkeye said. "The winner gets the honor of being the best agent—ever."

"Hmmm." Black Widow seemed doubtful.

"And breakfast . . . for a week," Hawkeye added.

"Deal," said Black Widow.

Hawkeye extended his hand to shake on it, but Black Widow was already off.

Hawkeye looked around. There'd been some rumors about strange lights deep in the woods. He decided to check it out. As he crept through the forest, he heard the buzzing and whirring of machines. Hawkeye slipped behind a large tree trunk and peeked around the side. He saw a squad of robots patrolling the edge of the woods, clearing a path toward the city with their lasers.

Huh, Hawkeye thought. *What kind of robot does landscaping?*

Hawkeye leapt up onto a nearby stump and drew an arrow.

"Hey, bug-bots—whatcha doing?"

The robots stopped and turned to face Hawkeye.

"Um . . . hello?" he said.

The robots all began firing at Hawkeye with their lasers.

He dove down and took cover. "Was it something I said?"

The blasts continued to hit the area around him. In rapid succession, he snapped one arrow after another at the robots. Soon there was only a pile of smoking metal rubble and sparking wires in the field.

Hawkeye called Black Widow on his wrist communicator. "I'm up to ten already, Natasha. Are you sure you don't want to quit?"

"I never quit," Natasha whispered. "But I have to call you back, Clint. I'm in the middle of something."

Black Widow knocked out some evil blue alien warriors. But when she looked down at the shadowy alley below, she saw a swarm of them advancing toward the city's harbor.

After taking a few running steps, Black Widow leapt off the roof into the mass of creatures below.

"Sorry to drop in unannounced," she said.

The warriors immediately surrounded her, but Black Widow didn't flinch. She moved in a blur, kicking, punching, and blasting the warriors out of her way until the alley was clear.

Her wrist comm rang again, just as the last warrior standing charged her.

"Hang on, Clint—it's going to take me a while to count up these guys," she said, before sweeping the warrior's leg and dropping him to the ground in two quick but powerful moves.

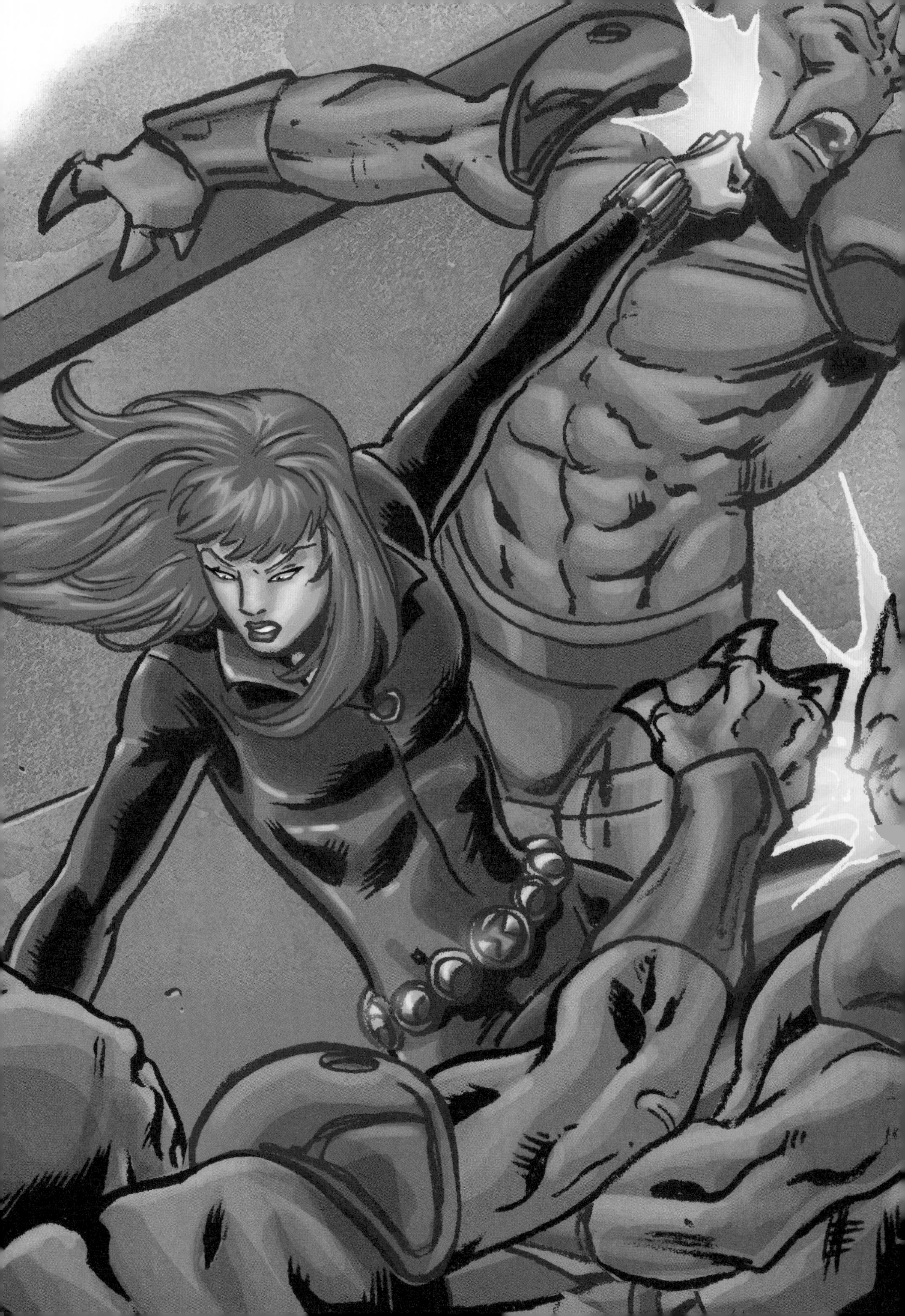

"Natasha! Clint!" Black Widow looked down at her wrist. Nick Fury was on the comm screen.

"We don't have time for games," Fury said. "We're getting reports of a multipoint alien invasion of the city."

"I just cleared a squad of robots in the forest," said Hawkeye.

Black Widow nodded. "And I just intercepted a troop of warriors in the warehouse district."

"So it's already begun," Fury said. "The communications are down. You need to get to S.H.I.E.L.D.'s heliport as soon as possible."

On Black Widow's motorcycle, she and Hawkeye scouted the downtown dockyards. Everything looked normal at first, but then the dockworkers began to attack! They were guards in disguise. The men charged toward Hawkeye and Black Widow.

"I'll drive," Black Widow shouted. "You clear a path."

Black Widow leaned forward and accelerated. As they drove through the cluster of guards, Hawkeye fired at the bad guys from the back of the bike. They saw a heavily guarded warehouse ahead.

"Looks like they infiltrated S.H.I.E.L.D.'s heliport," Black Widow said.

She skidded the bike to a halt. She and Hawkeye fought off the guards as they made their way to the door.

"Whatever they're hiding must be important," Hawkeye said as he fired arrows three at a time into the throng.

"Which means we need to find out what it is—" Black Widow knocked two brutes out of the way with an expert roundhouse kick.

"And stop it," Hawkeye finished for her. Together, the agents took down the guards one by one.

Suddenly, they heard a loud noise. "Natasha, the door!" Hawkeye pointed to a large loading dock, where a heavy steel gate was lowering. That was where they needed to go.

"Quick—get in, and I'll disable the alarms," he said.

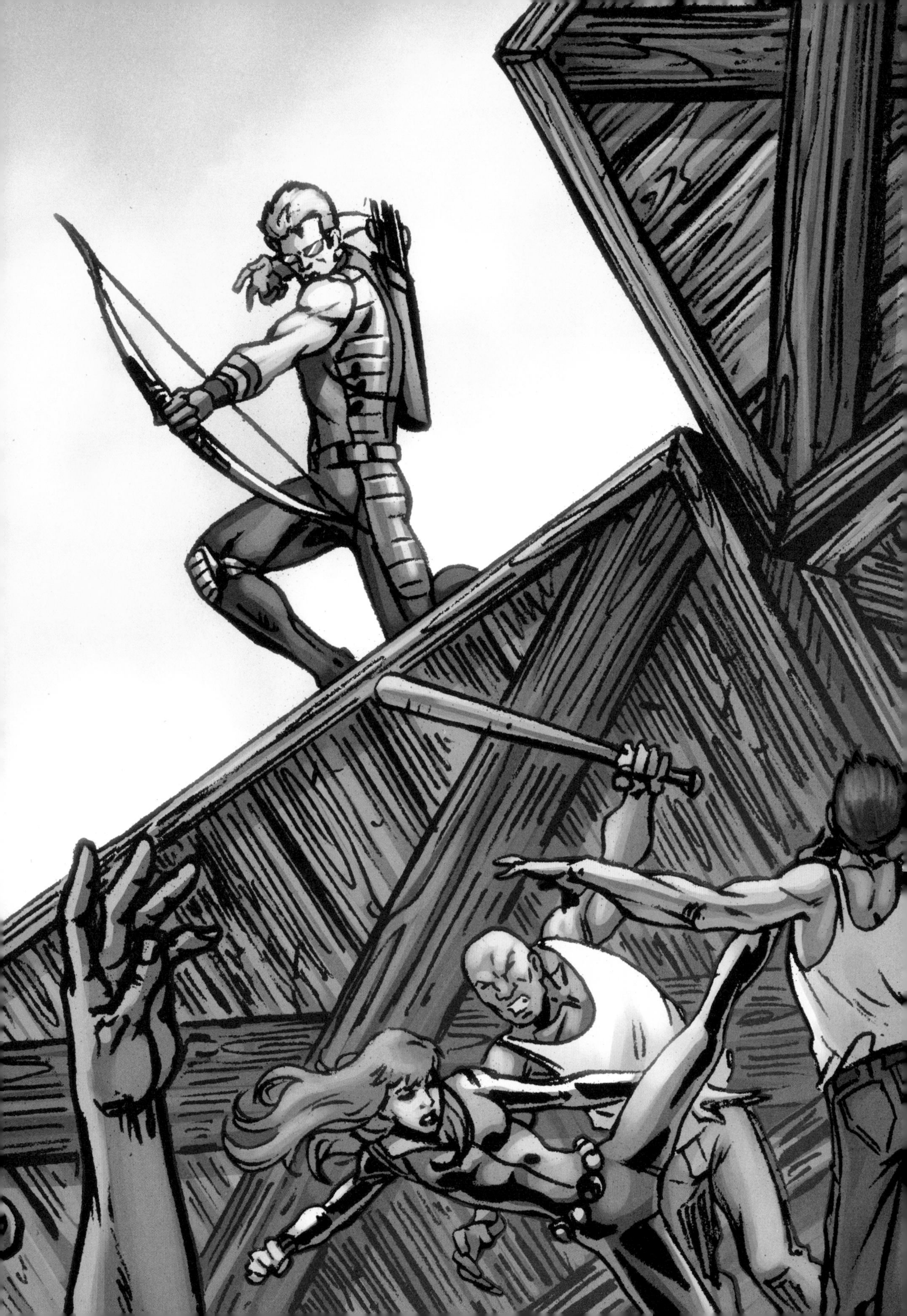

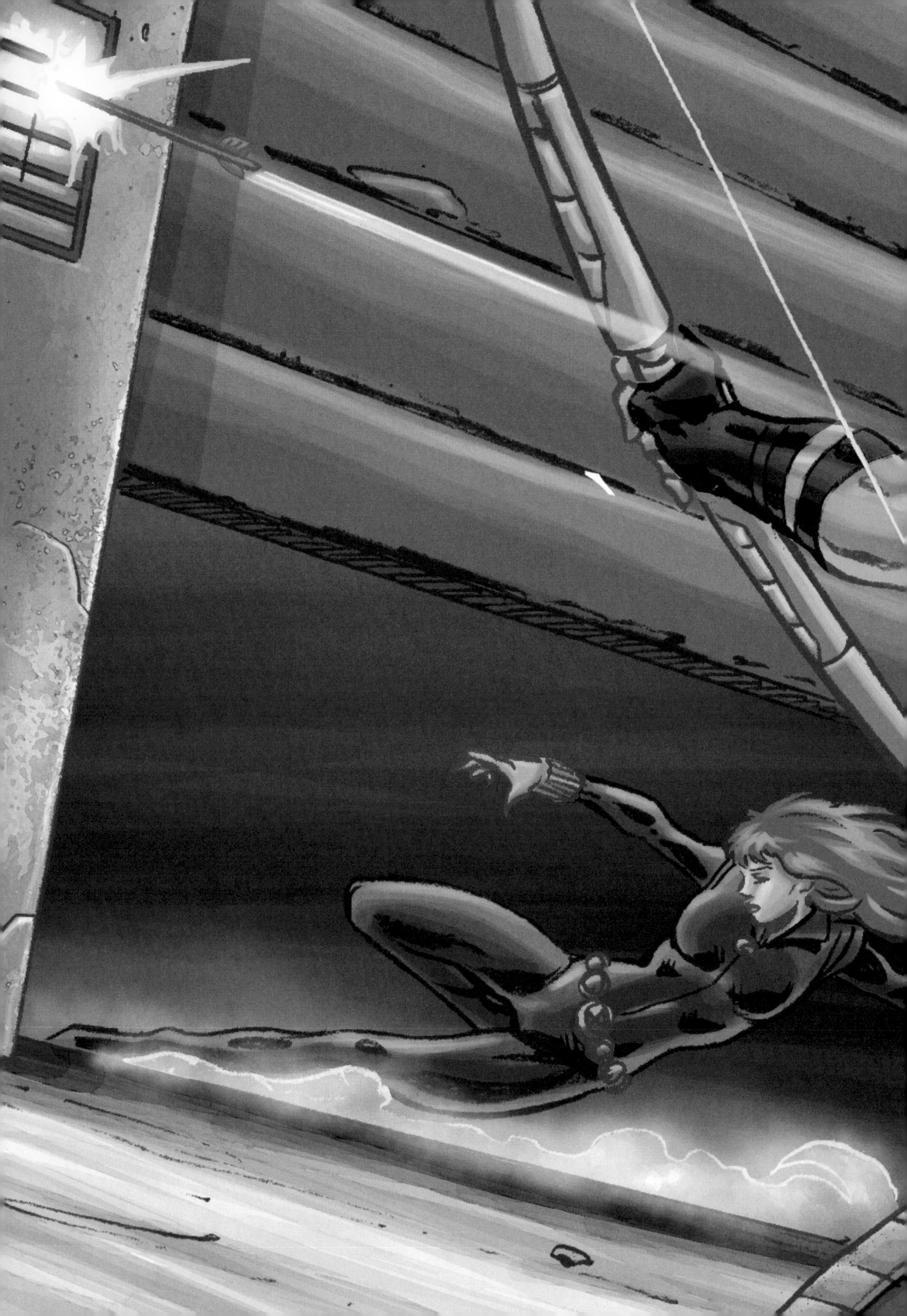

Black Widow nodded and dove under the closing gate while Hawkeye took out the alarm box with one precise shot.

Black Widow opened the door again for Hawkeye. Once inside, they crept down a long hall that led to a large door. Clint pointed toward the door, then held up two fingers, letting Natasha know there were two guards there.

Natasha nodded and suddenly leapt out into the middle of the hall. She blasted both guards at once.

"You could have left one for me," Hawkeye grumbled as he knelt down to hack the security pad.

Just then, Nick Fury called in with an update.

"Cap, Thor, and Iron Man are busy fighting aliens on the bridges and tunnels to keep them from spreading to the tristate area. You guys are in charge of shutting down the source. Got it, agents?"

"Got it!" Hawkeye and Black Widow replied.

The door slid open to reveal a courtyard, and Hawkeye and Black Widow both inhaled sharply. Hundreds of green brutes charged toward them.

"So are we still keeping a tally?" Black Widow yelled as she began to blast through the legion.

Clint counted off each arrow strike with a smile. "Twenty-two, twenty-three, twenty-four . . ."

After the invasion had been thwarted, Clint and Natasha returned to S.H.I.E.L.D. headquarters for debriefing.

"Great work!" Nick Fury said. "You are definitely the best."

Black Widow and Hawkeye glanced at each other. They didn't know whom Fury meant.

"That is, the best when you're working together," Fury added, giving them a stern look.

Black Widow and Hawkeye smiled at each other.

"I think we can agree on that," said Black Widow.

"Definitely," Hawkeye said. "But can we still get breakfast? I'm hungry!"

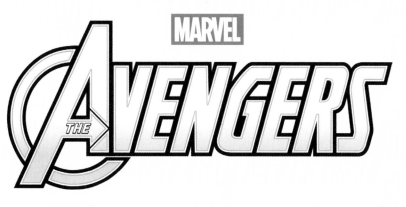

Practice Makes Perfect

Tony Stark was constantly inventing new types of Iron Man armor. Before breakfast, Tony might tinker with a suit that could withstand freezing temperatures. After lunch, he might perfect a suit that could move underwater. In his spare time, he might even doodle an idea for a suit that could go into outer space. He was like a kid with the coolest toy model kit money could buy.

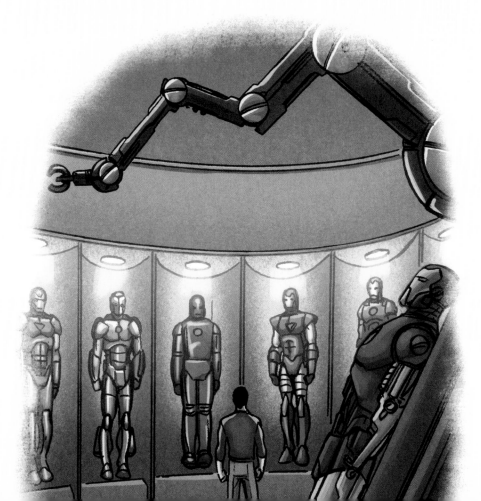

But Tony's latest suit could do something the others couldn't: snap itself together at his command. He stared at a dismantled suit on a nearby table and yelled, "Send me the arm!"

Instantly, a piece of the suit flew over and attached itself to Tony's hand and arm. "Now send the rest," he commanded. Other parts whizzed toward Tony, covering him piece by piece.

The voice-activated suit had attached itself to Tony in fifteen seconds flat.

"Not bad," he said with a satisfied nod. He'd been testing the suit's speed.

Just then, Crimson Dynamo smashed through the window of Tony's lab.

Crimson Dynamo also had a suit of armor, but he used his to commit crimes. The only thing that ever stood in the villain's way was Iron Man.

Dynamo had just broken out of jail. Now he would have his revenge on the man who had put him there in the first place.

"You must pay, Tony Stark," the Super Villain demanded.

"Sure," Tony began. "Cash or credit card?"

Annoyed at Tony's joke, Crimson Dynamo lunged forward. "Oh, not today . . . but soon," the evil villain snickered to himself. Iron Man didn't waste any time. He immediately beat back the metal monolith with his gauntlets.

It looked like Iron Man would stand triumphant. But Tony Stark wasn't the only one who'd given his costume an upgrade. Like Tony, Crimson Dynamo was also a brilliant inventor, and he had built in a new feature to his electrically powered suit. With the push of a blue button, he sent all his electrical current outward . . . into Tony's suit! Completely overloaded, Iron Man's metal shell short-circuited.

As Tony's suit began to shut down, Crimson Dynamo hurled Iron
Man into a wall.

"I don't understand," Tony said to his computer assistant,
J.A.R.V.I.S. "How is Crimson Dynamo able to do that with just the
push of a button?"

"Your suit can't handle that much power all at once," J.A.R.V.I.S.
responded.

Just before the suit turned off completely, Tony fired a weak
repulsor blast at Crimson Dynamo, but it was unable to stop the
villain. Crimson Dynamo left, cackling.

After Tony got back on his feet, he realized that Crimson Dynamo had done something before departing. He'd copied a computer file that contained some of Tony's blueprints. "Great," Tony told J.A.R.V.I.S. "Now he knows about all of my recent inventions, including how to make voice-activated armor."

Tony told his friend Rhodey that he was disappointed in himself. "I spent so long working on that voice-activated suit," he explained. "Then it just got shorted out in an instant. I'm so upset."

"And what do you do when you're upset?" Rhodey asked.

"I tinker," Tony answered.

"So tinker," Rhodey said. "Build an even *better* suit."

And that's just what Tony did. He worked tirelessly day and night, building the best suit possible. This outfit wouldn't be overloaded so easily, because it would have *double* the power supply of his previous costume. He also gave his new suit the ability to control other electronic devices. Crimson Dynamo had stolen the plans on Tony's computer, but he hadn't stolen Tony's newest plan, because it wasn't on his computer yet. It existed only in his head.

Just as Tony was putting the finishing touches on his new suit, his friend Pepper entered. She told him that Crimson Dynamo had just committed a robbery. When the police had captured him and taken off his armor, the vile villain had simply yelled, "Send me the suit!" and the suit had rebuilt itself all over his body. It was voice-activated armor! Dynamo had used the ideas he stole from Tony's computer. Tony decided it was time to take his new suit out for a test drive!

Just as Crimson Dynamo was about to rob another bank, Iron Man flew into view and blocked his path. Once again Crimson Dynamo tapped the blue button, and once again electrical current filled Tony's suit. But this time Iron Man's metal shell didn't short out. In fact, he kept charging toward the red rogue.

"How can this be?" Crimson Dynamo screamed, confused.

"Let's just say you're not the only one who gave your suit a makeover," Tony replied.

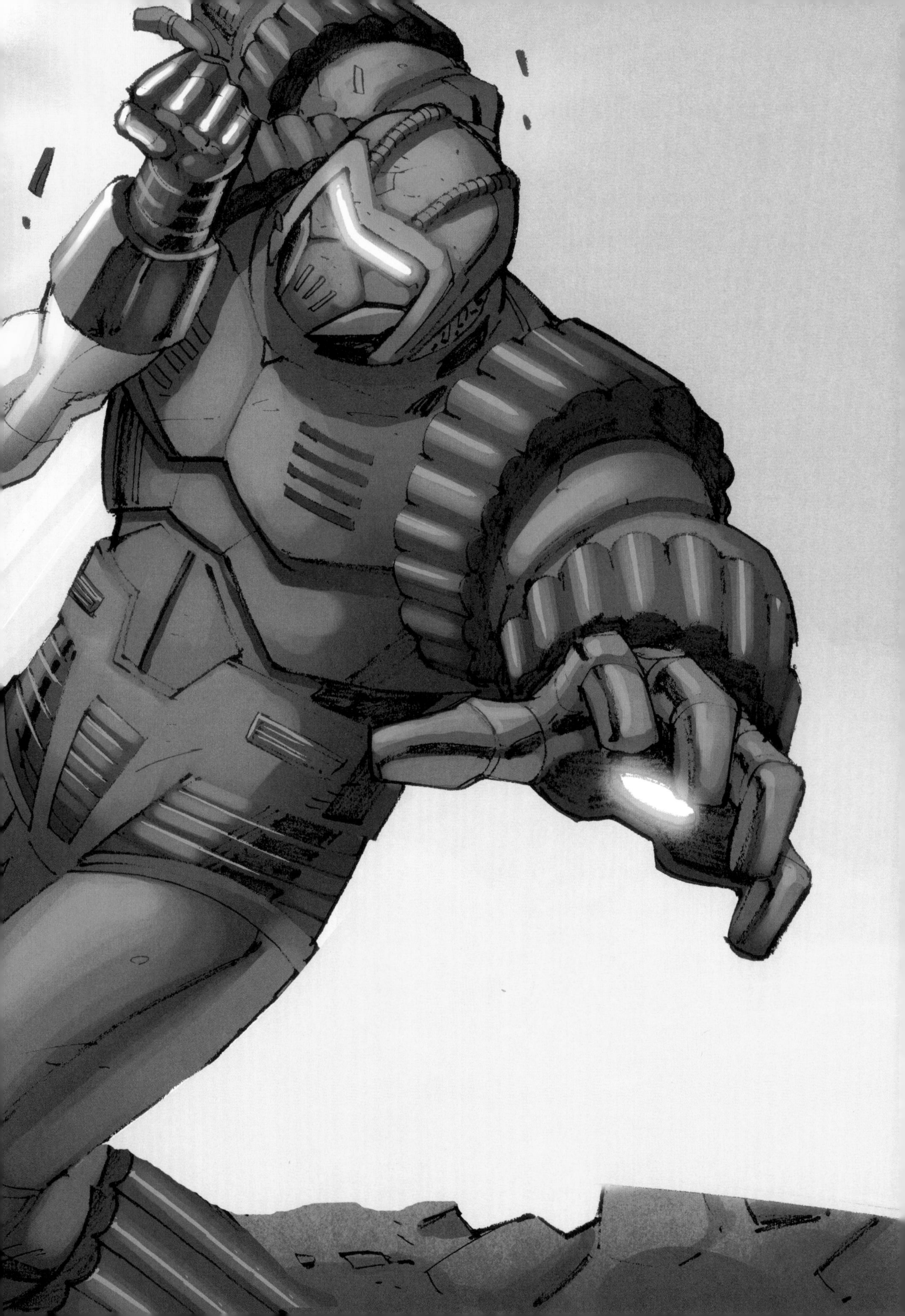

Now the tables were turned. Each time the Crimson Dynamo tried to short out Tony's suit, the Iron Man armor became stronger and stronger. His armor became more filled with energy. Just as the scarlet scoundrel was nervously trying to figure out a way to defeat Iron Man, the armored Avenger appeared before him . . . and *blasted* the villain with his chest unibeam. The Crimson Dynamo tried to get back up, but he found that he couldn't control his own suit. It wouldn't even move.

"I'm telling your costume to stay put," Tony explained. "My new outfit can control any electronic device, even yours. Oops. Did I forget to mention that?"

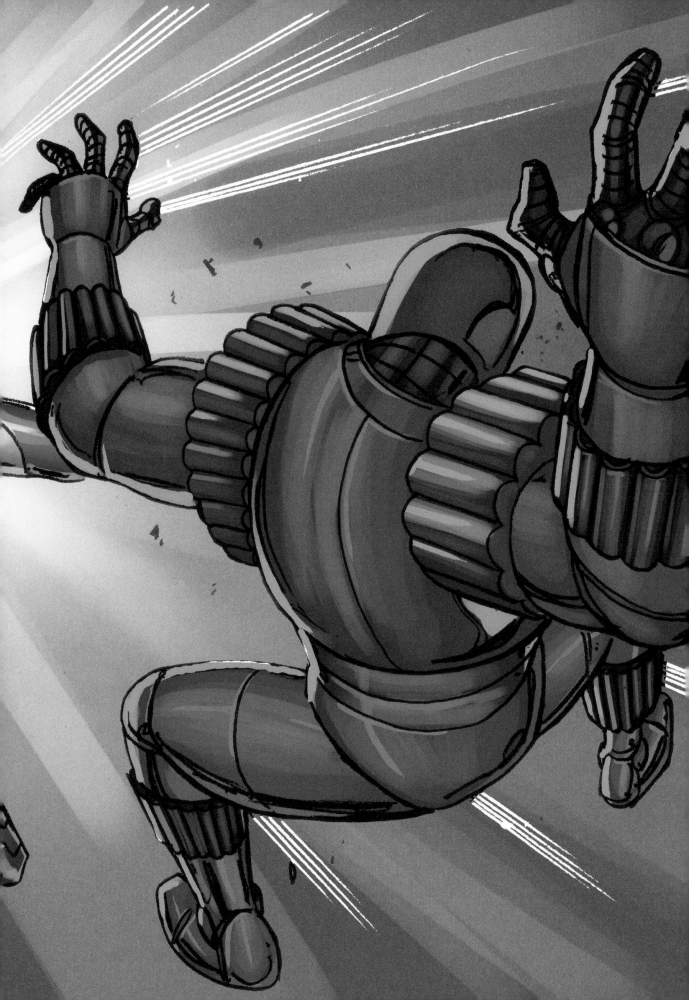

After the police took the Crimson Dynamo into custody, Tony got right back to work building an even better type of Iron Man suit. As he fiddled with a metal glove, he told J.A.R.V.I.S., "I really learned a lot today. You rarely get something right the first time you try it." Just then, he accidentally activated the glove's repulsor ray—and blasted a hole through the lab wall!

"You don't say," J.A.R.V.I.S. replied.

Dino Time

The Avengers had been very busy. Between dealing with the Taskmaster and thwarting another one of Loki's plots, they'd barely had time to sit back and relax.

Suddenly, Tony had an idea. "Why don't we build a time machine?"

"To go back in time and fight Loki again?" Bruce asked. "No, thank you."

"Not to go back in time," said Tony. "To slow down time. That way we can get some more rest before the next battle."

Bruce thought for a second. "Hmmm, that's actually not a bad idea—I'm in!"

The two of them went straight to work in Tony's lab. They couldn't wait to share their invention with the rest of the Avengers!

When they were done, Tony called Nick Fury to tell him the good news.

"It's our best invention yet," he said. "We're thinking of a cool name for it. Something snazzy, like the Machine of Time."

"How about the *Mistake* of Time?" Fury replied, pointing at the window to a disturbance in Central Park. "It looks like your little machine may have opened a portal to another time period!"

"Really? Wow, this thing is even better than I thought," Tony said. "I wonder what time period the portal leads to."

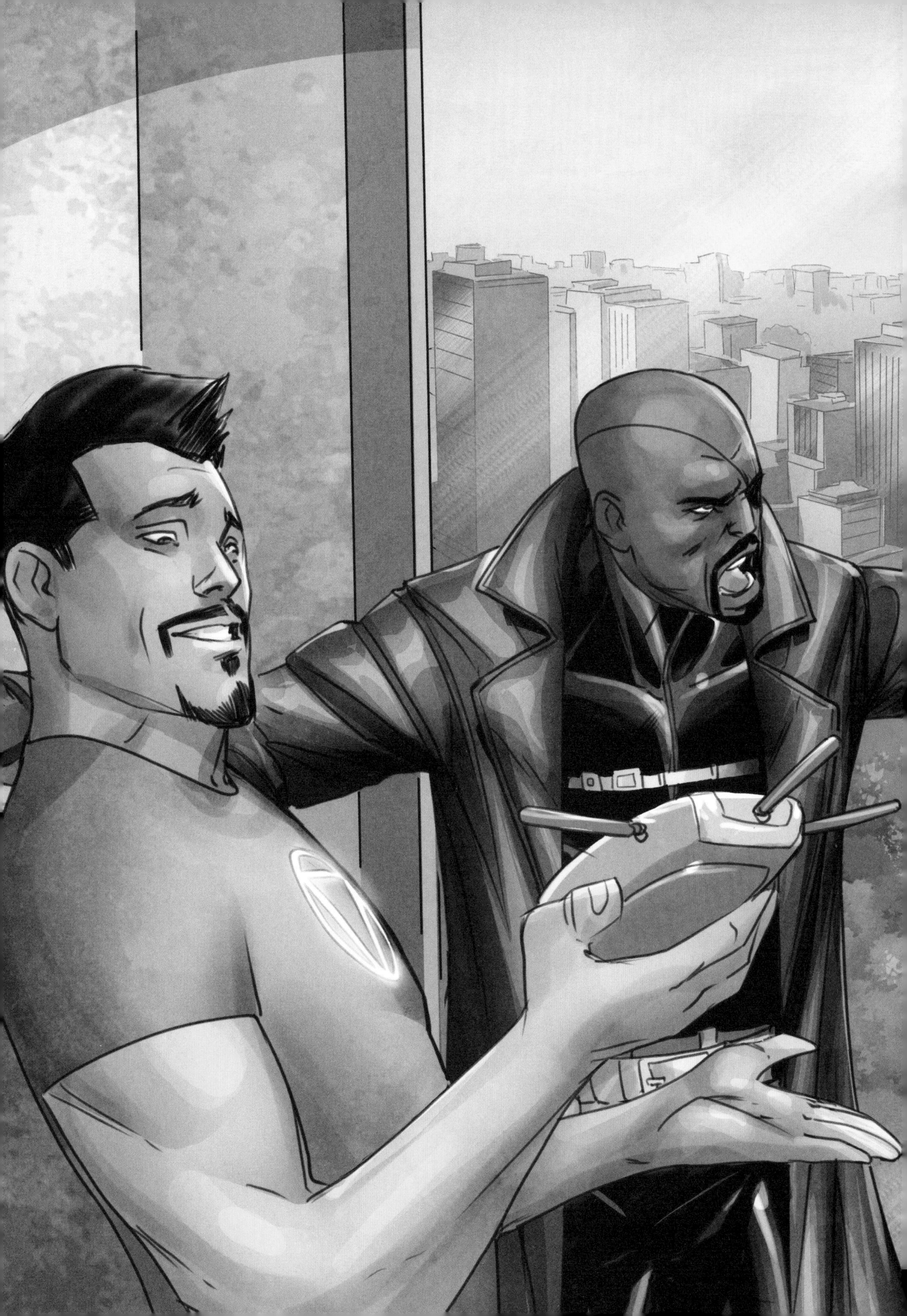

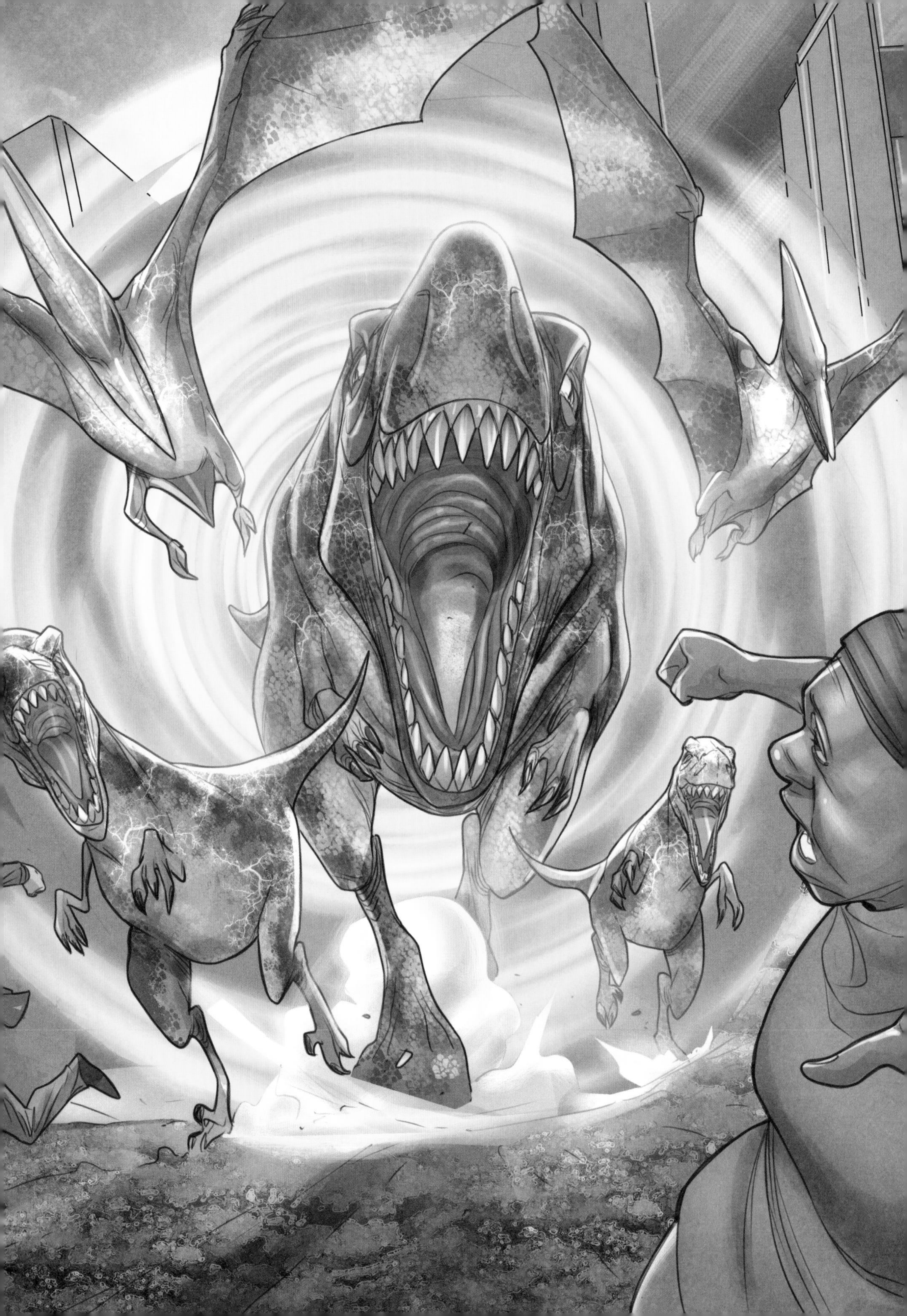

Tony soon got his answer: the Cretaceous period. Basically, lots of very big dinosaurs!

All the people in Central Park ran screaming in different directions as a *T. Rex* came crashing through the portal. Velociraptors raced along the grass while shrieking pterodactyls swooped through the air.

Fury glared at Tony. "Whatever you did, you better fix it quick, before I get really mad."

"Guess I'll start by getting *Bruce* really mad," Tony said.

Moments later, Iron Man and the Hulk were racing toward the dinosaurs in Central Park.

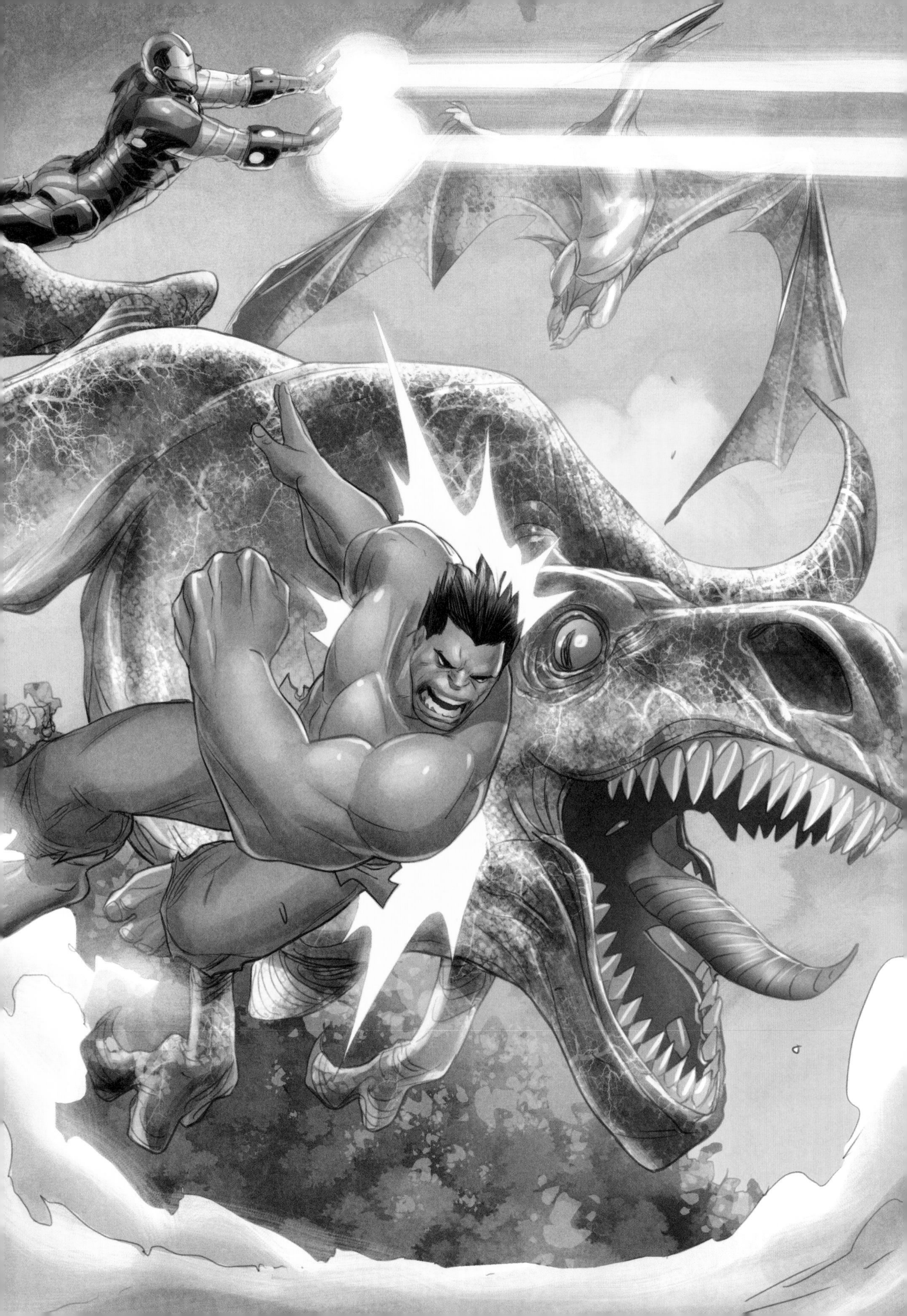

"I'm starting to see why these things went extinct," Iron Man said, firing two repulsor beams at an incoming pterodactyl. "They're not very sophisticated creatures, are they—?"

"Hulk *SMASH*!" yelled the green Avenger, slamming his body into a *T. Rex*.

Iron Man shook his head. "You know what, never mind."

The two Avengers fought valiantly, but more and more dinosaurs kept coming through the portal. Soon Iron Man and the Hulk were hopelessly outnumbered.

Iron Man was about to blast another pterodactyl when a raptor chomped down on his arm, causing the beam to misfire.

"A little help here!" Iron Man called out.

Hulk started to come to his aid, but a swarm of dinosaurs attacked him at that moment. He was surrounded!

"Wasn't our time machine supposed to give us a little more rest and relaxation?" Iron Man said. "This isn't exactly what I had in mind!"

The two Super Heroes were still struggling against the dinosaurs when a tricolored beam shot through the sky, scattering them so Hulk could muscle through.

Hulk barely had time to get out of the way before another powerful beam caused a small explosion, sending dinosaurs flying in multiple directions.

Iron Man freed himself and flew up into the air, where he was able to see the source of the explosive beam.

It was Thor who had sent the lightning bolt through the air. He and the rest of the Avengers had come to help!

"Fury said you guys were getting some rest and relaxation," said Captain America. "Looks like you could use a hand."

Iron Man smiled as he saw the other Avengers. "Oh, you know me," he said. "I can never sit still for too long."

"I know," Cap said. "Sometimes I wish you would."

Thor raised his mighty hammer. "Well, now is not the time for sitting. Now is the time for hunting. Who's with me?"

The battle was much more evenly matched with the other Avengers there. Hulk looked around and ran toward a nearby baseball field.

Iron Man called after him: "Really, Hulk? This is no time to be playing games."

But Hulk wasn't playing.

He grabbed the metal fence that enclosed the field and tore it loose. He held it up as the other Avengers guided the dinosaurs toward it, and then he wrapped it around the dinosaurs and sealed them in. With one gigantic heave, Hulk swung the entire package back through the portal, which contracted and disappeared with an ear-splitting pop.

"Now that's what I call a home run," Iron Man said.

After all the dinosaurs had been taken care of and the Avengers had cleaned up the city, Tony and Bruce locked the time machine in the basement.

"Hey, I think I know where we went wrong," Tony said. "All this time, we were trying to slow down time to get some more rest. What we should be doing is speeding up time so our battles can go faster."

Bruce just shook his head and smiled. "Okay, I'm in."

Not Easy Being Big and Green

Being the Hulk must be incredible. He is one of Earth's Mightiest Heroes. He can lift a boulder ten times his weight. His thunderclap can make the loudest *BOOM*. Watch out when he bangs his fists against the ground! His battle cry is known throughout the world as "Hulk *SMASH*!" Who would not want to be the Hulk?

Though the Hulk is a hero, people are afraid of him. Every day, when he walks down the street, mothers hold their kids tighter at the sight of him. Strangers stare at the Hulk in fear, sometimes with their mouths open in shock at his appearance. Hulk tries his best to ignore the looks. Yet he can't help but feel a little sad when people call him mean names.

"Look at that monster over there!" a man shouted.

"Jim, stop it. You don't want to upset the monster," whispered the man's friend.

Deep down, Hulk felt hurt and lonely.

"Hulk sad," he mumbled to himself.

People don't know how to treat the Hulk, because he looks different from them. They just don't understand what it's like to be different.

But that day was worse than usual. When Jim called him a monster, Hulk wanted to prove to everyone he was good. But all that hurt and anger made it hard for Hulk to control his feelings, and he got an urge to smash everything!

"Hulk *SMASH*!" he roared, and turned around. Hulk wrecked the pavement and made a big mess. Shocked and terrified, everyone stared at the Hulk.

"See, I told you he was a monster," Jim muttered.

Hulk felt so misunderstood!

Embarrassed, Hulk decided to walk down a different street. As he made his way through the city, he heard a little girl crying. At first he thought she was upset because of the way he looked, but then he noticed a kitten stuck in a tree.

"Little girl want kitty?" Hulk asked the child.

"Please! I don't know how to get my kitty down," she cried.

Hulk reached his hand into the tree and helped get the pet back to its owner. The girl gasped with joy. "Thank you, Hulk!" Hulk realized a tiny ounce of kindness could go a long way. He knew he could be good. He didn't have to be the monster Jim thought he was.

Just then, Hulk got a call on his Avengers communicator!

"The Avengers need your help right now," said S.H.I.E.L.D. director Nick Fury.

"Hulk ready!" he shouted.

Excited to prove himself as a hero again, Hulk rushed to join his mighty friends. The Avengers were on a mission in outer space against the most powerful villain of all: Thanos!

When Thanos attacked the moon, each Avenger took off in a different direction to battle his Outriders, but the Hulk wanted only one thing: to smash Thanos!

Hulk took on Thanos head-to-head and caught the villain with a surprise punch.

"Hulk make Thanos pay!" he shouted.

Thanos and the Outriders were finally defeated. Hulk tried to remember he could be a hero no matter what people might call him—and that he could use his strength for good.

Soon afterward, Hulk spotted Jim and his friend from earlier that day. He heard Jim calling him a monster again and felt his anger boiling up inside. He wanted to smash something . . . badly. But he knew he shouldn't.

"Hulk no smash," Hulk said to himself.

Suddenly, out of nowhere, a truck came flying down the street, heading straight for the name-callers! Hulk leapt out and stopped the truck from hitting them.

Despite all the mean things they had said about him, Hulk still protected the men. Jim was shocked that the Hulk had come to his rescue.

"You saved all our lives! Thank you, Hulk!" said the truck driver. He explained, "The Absorbing Man is wreaking havoc over there, and I was so scared that I drove away fast and lost control!"

Hulk didn't have a moment to waste. He knew what he had to do. He raced down the block and saw the Absorbing Man attacking citizens! "Hulk angry!" he grunted. He hated when bullies picked on innocent people. He knew that was the right thing to get angry about. The green Goliath sprang into action! Without thinking, he crashed through a wall to stop the Absorbing Man in his tracks. "HULK SMASH!" he yelled.

"You're wasting your time—you'll never defeat me!" the Absorbing Man said with a laugh.

As the Hulk lunged at the enemy, he suddenly heard a voice from behind him: "My spidey-sense was tingling! Need a hand, buddy?" It was Spider-Man!

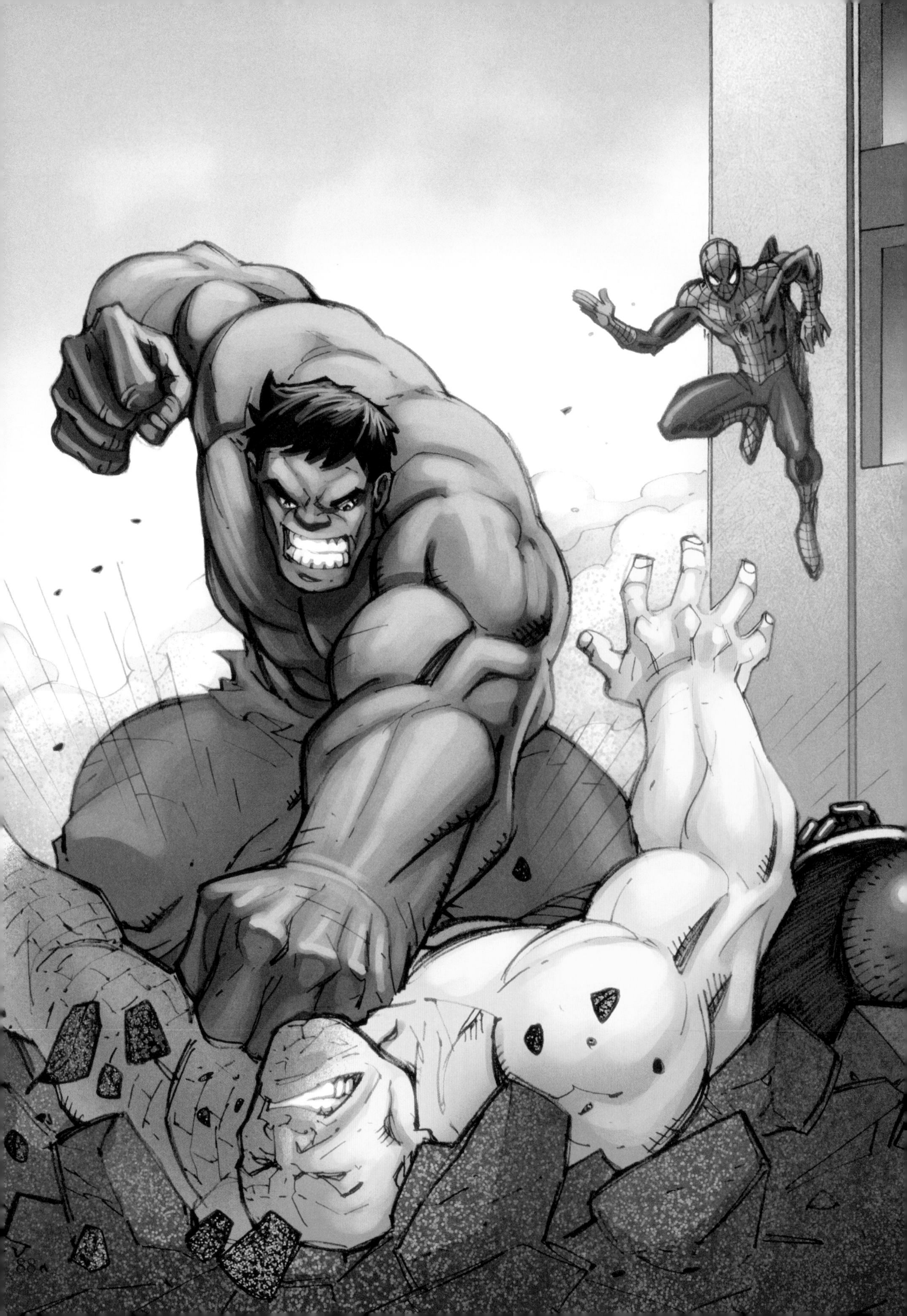

Hulk was surprised to get help, but he welcomed it. When the Hulk and Spider-Man put their strength together for good, no villain could win!

"Absorbing Man no match for Hulk and little spider!" Hulk shouted.

With Spider-Man's help, the Hulk stopped the Absorbing Man. Hulk enjoyed being part of a team. The people who were mean to the Hulk now looked at the big green hero with awe. They began to realize they were wrong about how they had treated him.

Hulk clobbered the bad guy with one mighty punch after another.

"So I think you got a handle on this. Should I just cheer from the sidelines?" Spidey joked.

After Spidey webbed the Absorbing Man to the ground for the cops, Hulk shook hands with Spider-Man and headed back to the Avengers Tower, his home.

Hulk was starting to feel that he was good, but he knew
he could be even better. Hulk worked with his friends to be
stronger than before. Black Widow and Hawkeye helped
Hulk with his training and weight lifting.

"Hulk strong!" he shouted. Hawkeye was a little worried,
but he knew his friend would not hurt him.

Hulk was happy to be home, where his friends did not call him names or look at him like he was weird. They treated him like a normal person, and that was just what Hulk had always wanted.

"I saw you knock out Thanos, but can you win in an arm-wrestling match against me?" Thor teased.

"I'm rooting for Hulk!" Falcon said with a laugh.

Hulk grinned.

Hulk learned that even though some people continued to find him scary, he was still happy to have his powers, because he used them for good. And for the times when he forgot what made him great, he would always have his friends around to remind him.

After a long day of fighting alongside the Avengers and Spider-Man, rescuing a child's kitty, and even helping his bullies when they were in need, Hulk realized something else:

"Hulk hungry!"

Lending a Wing

Usually, people noticed Sam Wilson, especially when he was Falcon. But Sam hoped that wouldn't be the case that day. He had gone undercover to expose a crime ring. He was pretending to be one of the bad guys to catch them in the act. He made sure to dress the part so he did not stand out. That way, nobody would suspect he was secretly an Avenger!

But when he left to meet the crooks, his pet falcon, Redwing, followed him. At the meeting, Redwing circled around Sam. A burly blond thief named Hoyt pointed at Sam's feathered friend and yelled, "Hey, that's Redwing, Falcon's pet bird!" Then he stared at Sam and said, "That means *you're* the Falcon!" Oh, no! Sam's sting operation was not going as planned!

Suddenly, Hoyt and the other crooks surrounded Falcon and Redwing. Hoyt turned to his pals and growled, "Looks like we caged the Falcon, boys." Aided by Redwing's sharp talons, Sam fought his way out of the den of thieves. The duo were outnumbered, but they were trained for tough situations like that, even without Sam's Falcon suit.

Falcon and Redwing led the crooks on a lengthy chase. The heroes soon found themselves backed into an alley.

Hoyt and his men were getting tired. Sam, on the other hand, had saved his strength. He felt that the fight was finally about to go his way.

Hoyt jeered, "What are you gonna do now, fly away?"

But before Sam could say anything, Captain America suddenly appeared in front of him in a flash of red, white, and blue. Cap's shield formed a wall between the heroes and the gang of thieves. "Sorry I'm late." Cap grinned at Sam. "Traffic was terrible."

Without a moment's hesitation, Captain America landed a strong right hook across Hoyt's jaw, sending him flying. With Cap's help, Sam and Redwing captured the thieves and turned them over to the police.

Later, at Avengers Tower, Sam clearly had something on his mind. When he and Captain America sat down to lunch, Sam moped and picked at his sandwich.

"Everything okay?" Cap asked.

"Sure," Sam said with a shrug. He excused himself and headed for the gym.

Captain America noticed something was off with Sam. He stood in the gym doorway and watched Sam jab at a punching bag in frustration. "Good team-up earlier," Cap said, trying to cheer his friend up.

But Sam didn't reply at first. The room was full of the sound of Sam's quick jabs to the punching bag, which were growing even louder.

Finally, Sam mumbled, "I didn't need your help in that alley. I was doing fine on my own." He trudged away, leaving Cap stunned. Cap had only wanted to help his friend, not upset him.

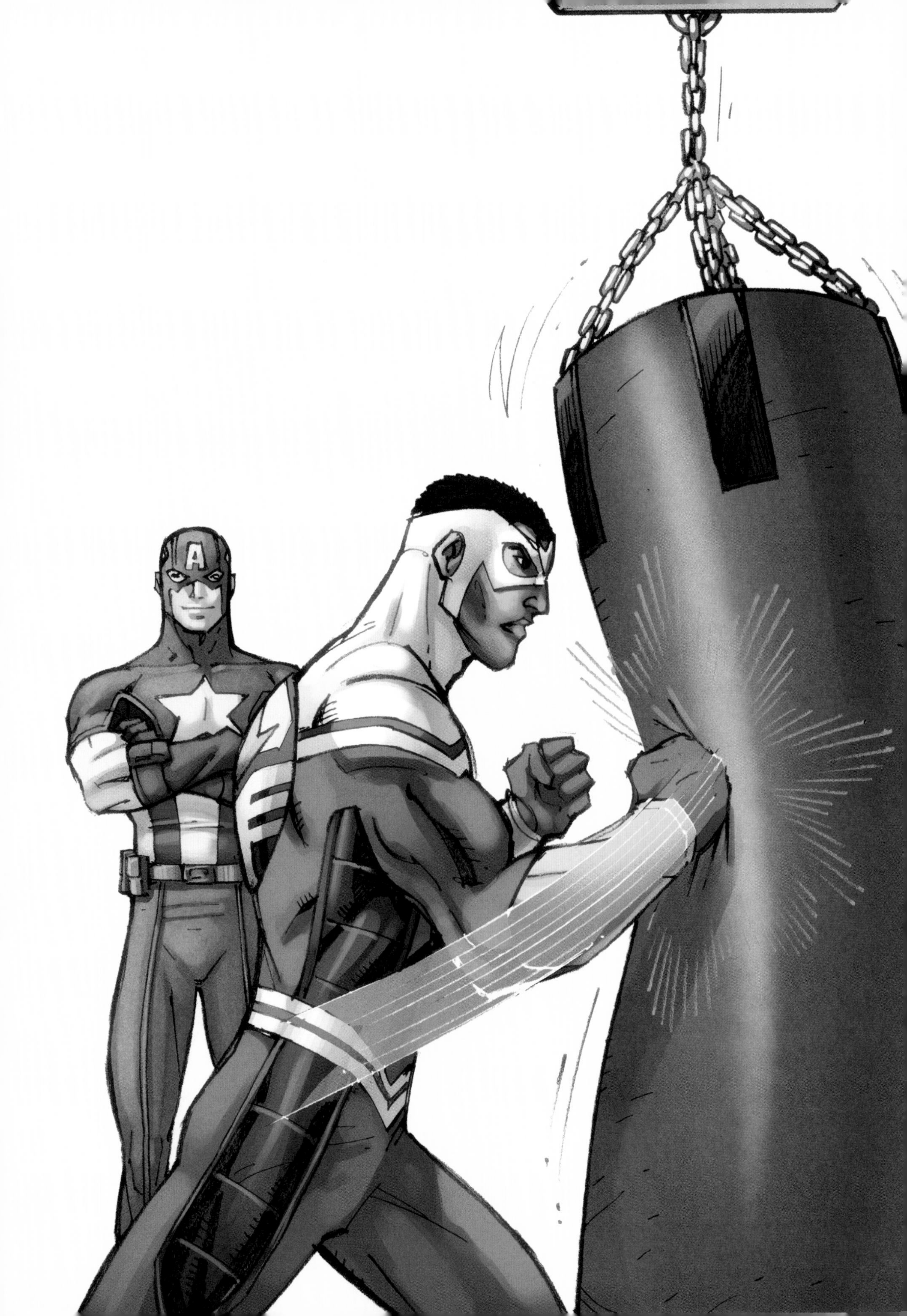

Falcon felt cooped up. He needed to clear his head. Some people do that by taking a walk, but not Sam. He took to the air, flying over New York. As he soared high above the clouds, Sam muttered, "*Real* heroes don't need to be rescued." But the longer he flew, the more he realized he shouldn't have been so rude to Cap.

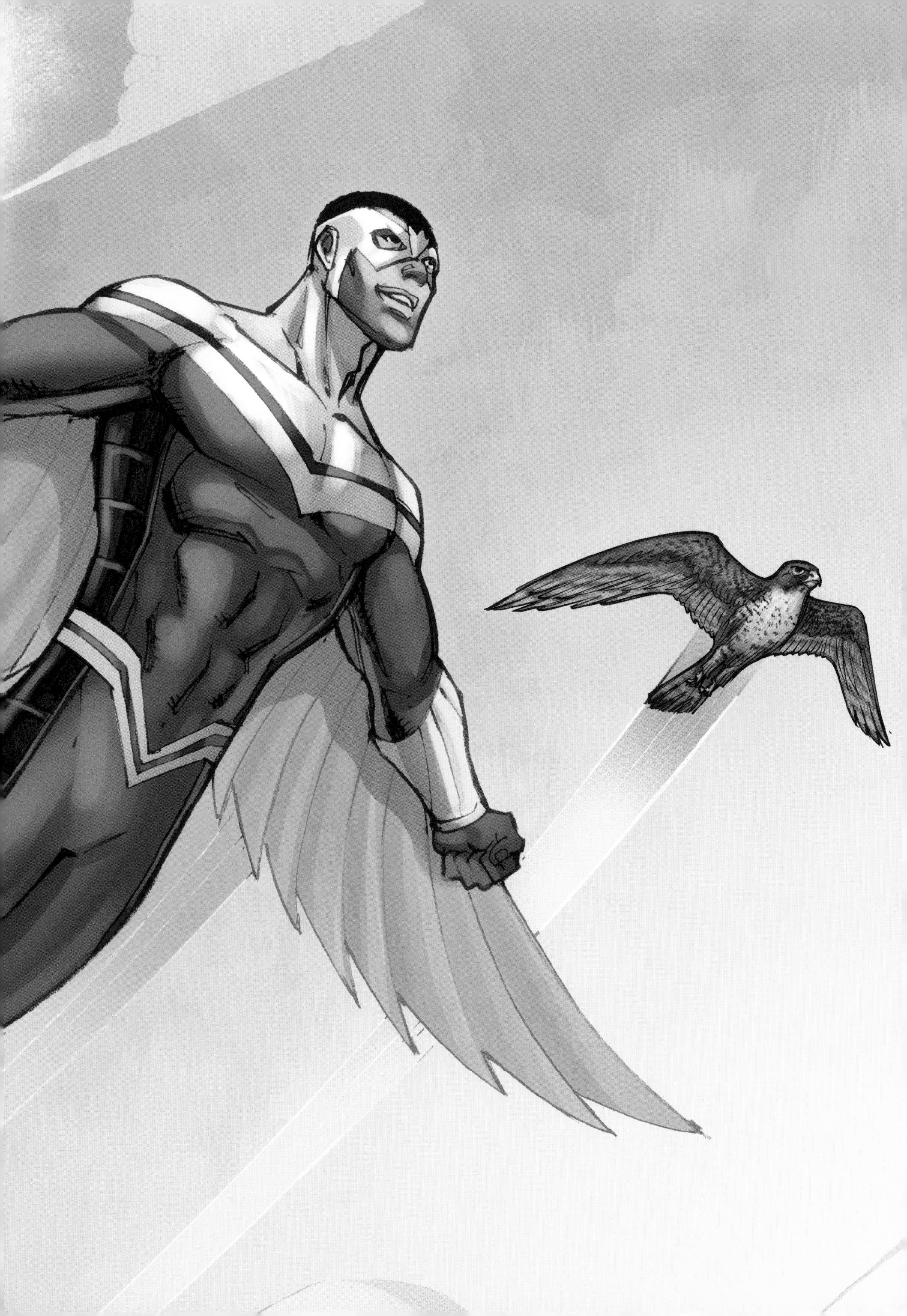

Just then, Falcon received an emergency message from Black Widow. Captain America needed their help. Sam couldn't believe his ears. "Why would *Cap* need help?" he asked when he met up with Widow.

"*Everyone* needs a helping hand from time to time," she said. "*Even* a Super-Soldier."

Falcon perched on a tree branch. He could see Captain America on a rooftop . . . surrounded by Hydra agents! Sam silently gestured toward Black Widow, who was hidden nearby. It was time to spring into action! Black Widow kept the Hydra goons distracted with her fast and furious fighting style so they wouldn't see Sam flying toward them.

When Falcon had nearly reached Cap, a Hydra agent strapped on a jet pack and took off—with Cap in his evil clutches! At lightning speed, Sam flew after him. He chased the airborne Hydra spy tirelessly, zigzagging through the air. Finally, Sam flew circles around the agent until his enemy was dizzy. Falcon knocked out the green-clad goon with a thundering *THWACK!*

Oh, no! Sam realized that the unconscious villain had let go of Cap! The star-spangled Avenger was plummeting toward the roof below. With only seconds to spare, the winged warrior swooped down and caught Cap! Falcon felt pretty good about helping Captain America for a change.

Sam lowered the powerful patriot to the roof just in time for Cap to hurl his shield at a horde of Hydra operatives. They fell to the ground like a row of bowling pins. It was truly a *strike* against Hydra!

Now that they were working together, Falcon, Black Widow, and Captain America quickly defeated the Hydra agents who were still standing. The Avengers captured the enemy spies, proving that Earth's Mightiest Heroes were even more heroic as a team.

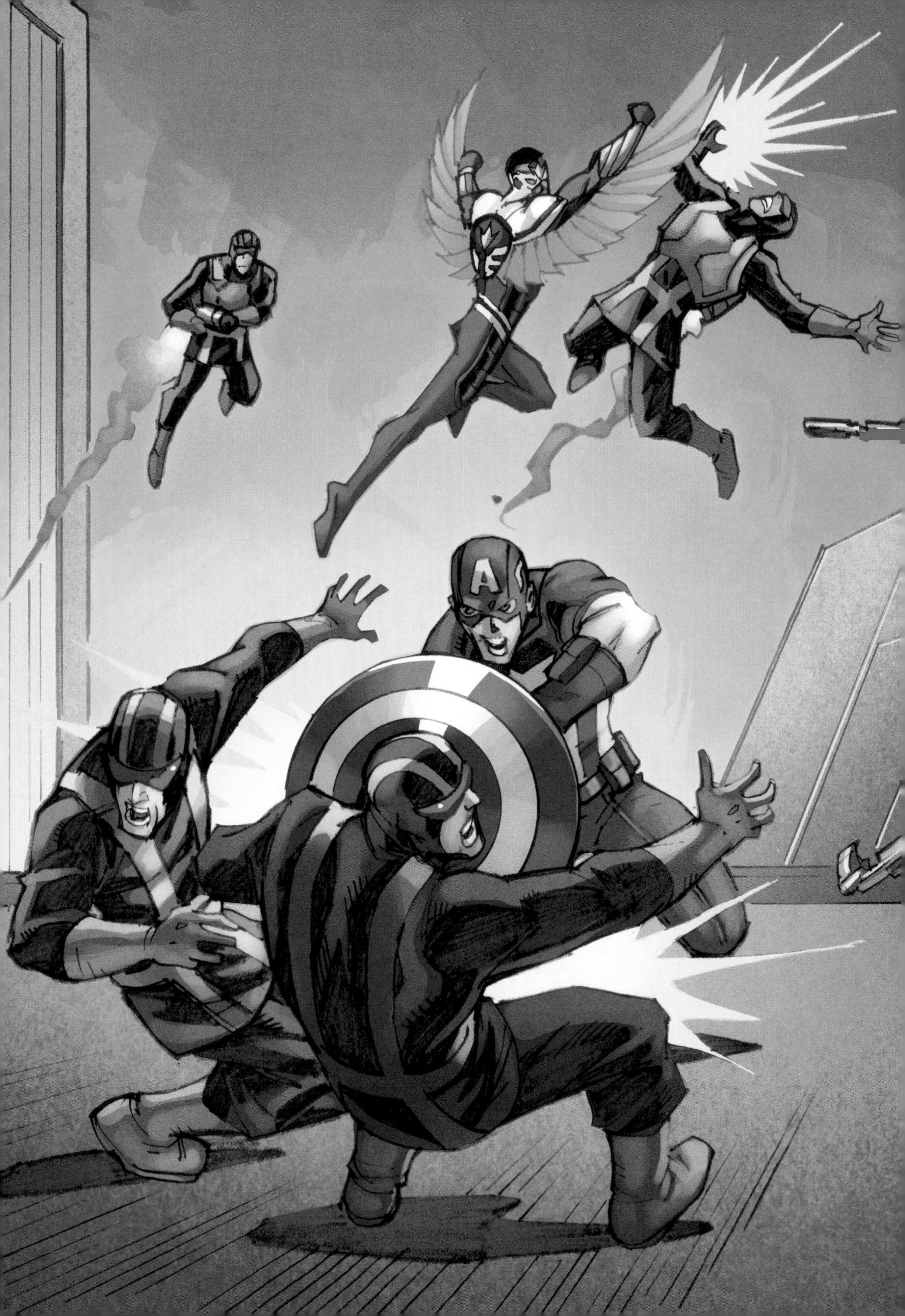

Afterward, Falcon, Cap, and Black Widow got together with the other Avengers to celebrate their victory. Sam told Cap, "Sorry for the way I acted earlier. If you hadn't given me a hand back in that alley . . ."

Captain America smiled. "Don't sweat it, Sam," he said.

"You know," Sam told his teammates, "I learned a tough lesson today. *Real* bravery is admitting when you need help."

Sam looked at his friends. He knew they had his back, and that he had theirs. And that made Sam feel like the luckiest person in the world!

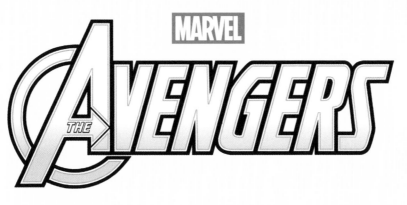

Calling All Avengers!

There came a day when Earth's Mightiest Heroes needed help. That day, there were *two* threats at the same time!

The Avengers were busy fighting the Wrecker and his Wrecking Crew—a superpowered group that loved destruction. Sometimes they just wanted to knock down buildings!

Meanwhile, Hydra—an evil group determined to rule the world—was setting its newest plan in motion! But with the Avengers busy battling the Wrecking Crew, who was going to stop Hydra?

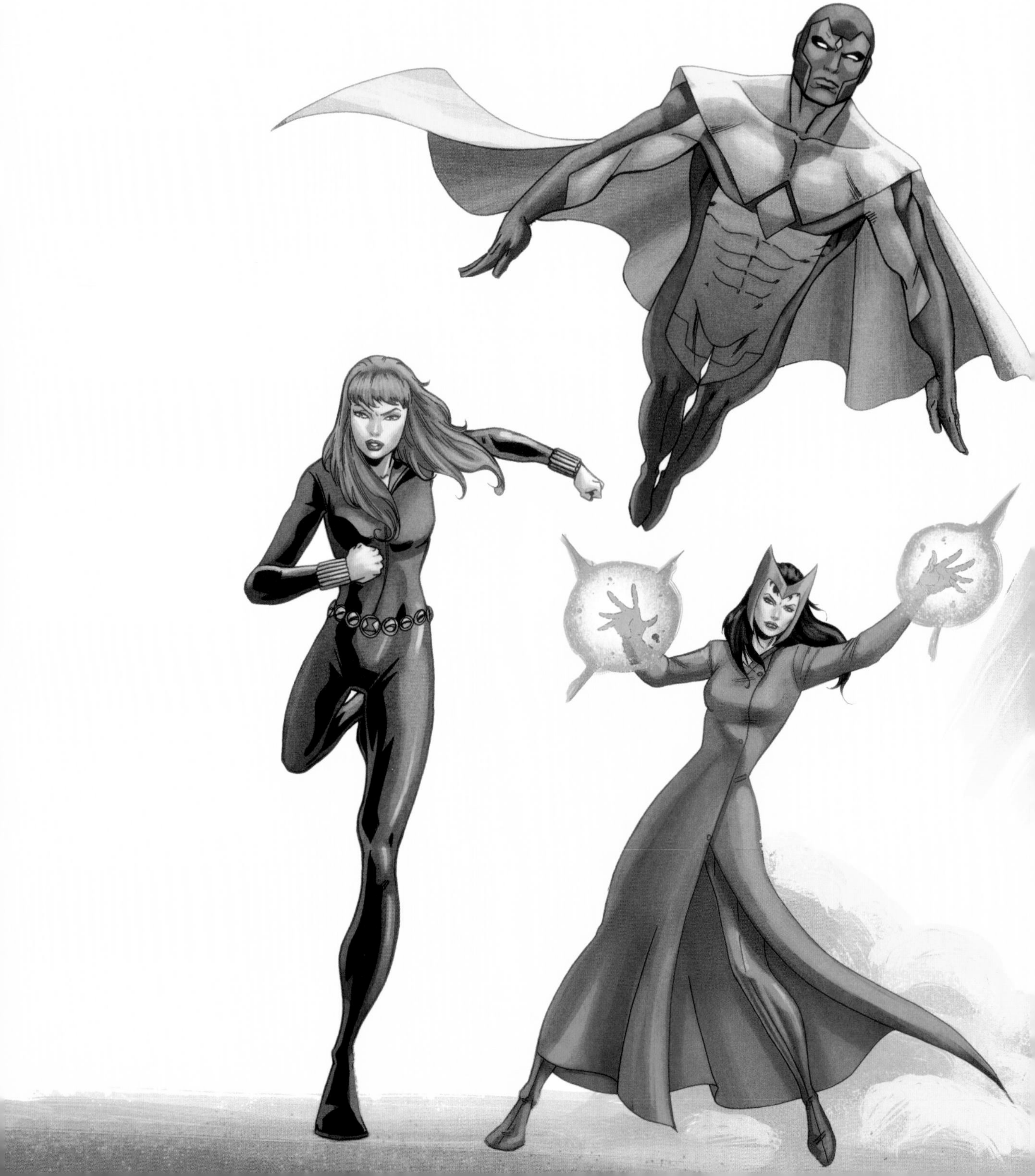

Captain America suggested calling in the new recruits.

Iron Man said, "They're not ready yet!"

Captain America thought Iron Man was wrong, but he knew the original Avengers thought less of the new Avengers—just because they were new to the team! "We should give them a shot," Cap said.

Meet the newest members of the Avengers. Falcon!
Vision! Scarlet Witch! Hawkeye! Quicksilver! And the super spy
Black Widow!

Falcon had been Captain America's partner for a long time. He was really Sam Wilson, a S.H.I.E.L.D. agent with a supercool flight suit that came complete with wings. He was one of the few people with the skills and strength to use the flight suit, and when he did—bad guys, beware! Falcon could swoop down from the sky and stop crime.

Falcon flew so fast that he could get anywhere in the city in just a few minutes! He had fought Hydra many times with Captain America, so he was a great Avenger to have on a mission against that group. Always a friendly face, Falcon was often the first team member to offer a helping hand.

When Captain America called about Hydra, Falcon asked only, "When do we get started?"

Among the new recruits was Vision. He was an android, which is a funny way of saying he was a robot that looked human. Robots don't need the same things humans need. As a robot, Vision didn't have to eat or sleep, but he did have to power up.

He had many special abilities. He could control his density. That meant he could walk through walls or become as hard as a diamond! He could also shoot beams from his eyes and fly, and he was super strong.

But what made him an Avenger was his heroic spirit. He was one robot with heart!

Vision was the next to receive Captain America's call about Hydra. "Incoming call from Captain America! Time to get the other Avengers!" said Vision, ready to jump into action.

At the Avengers Tower, Falcon and Vision went to get Scarlet Witch. They found her floating in a ball of her own mystical energy!

"Whoa! What are you doing?" Falcon asked her.

"There are more threats to the world than the ones you can punch, Falcon," Scarlet Witch said. "I'm fighting those threats right now."

Falcon didn't understand what exactly Scarlet Witch's powers were, but he knew that she could make the impossible happen. He thought she might prove to be the most powerful Avenger of all—and since his friends were Iron Man, Hulk, and Thor, that was really saying something!

"It appears we're needed," Scarlet Witch said. "Let's get my brother!"

Just as Scarlet Witch mentioned her brother, the communicator came to life with his voice. "I'm on my way," Quicksilver shouted through the speaker.

Quicksilver was the fastest man on the planet! He was able to run at super speed. Just then, he was outrunning a super-fast train on his way to meet his fellow Avengers! Quicksilver also knew how talented and powerful he was. Of all the Avengers, he was the one who most enjoyed being a celebrity.

Captain America's call also came through the training room where Hawkeye was practicing with his bow and arrows. Hawkeye had such good eyesight that he could see his targets from far away—and then hit them!

His bow had many different kinds of arrows—ones that caught fire, ones that cooled things off, ones with nets, and many more. While Hawkeye had no powers, he had proven that he was able to keep up with his superpowered friends just fine.

Completing her training session with Hawkeye, Black Widow was jumping through a maze of laser beams. She was a very skilled gymnast. "Looks like Cap needs our help, Hawkeye!" Black Widow finished her flips through the maze and landed, ready for combat.

Black Widow asked Hawkeye, "Do you think they're ready to accept us as Avengers, or do they still think of us as the new members?"

Hawkeye knew that Black Widow felt like she wasn't really part of the team—and sometimes he felt that way, too. "It just takes time, Widow," Hawkeye said, hoping it would cheer her up a little.

As they joined the others, she set her Widow's Bite gauntlets on stun. Those wrist zappers really did pack a wallop!

As soon as the Avengers saw Hydra's goons, Black Widow yelled out to them, "Surrender now, Hydra. This is your one and only warning!"

The Hydra agent in charge laughed at them and said, "You're not even the real Avengers! There's no way we'd surrender to you!"

But just because they were newer to the team didn't mean they weren't as good as the original Avengers. They made sure Hydra wouldn't have the chance to underestimate them again!

After wrapping up the Hydra
agents, the new Avengers went
to help the rest of the Avengers
fight the Wrecking Crew! As
it turned out, the original
Avengers needed some
extra power!

Scarlet Witch called out a spell of protection that saved Captain America, Thor, and Hulk. The other new Avengers took down the villains! Iron Man couldn't believe he had been wrong about his new teammates.

With only the Wrecker left standing, Captain America and Quicksilver were able to take care of him—together! "There will be no more destruction today, Wrecker," Captain America cried.

"Or ever again," Quicksilver added.

POW! POW! The fists of two mighty heroes were more than enough to knock out the Wrecker!

While saving the city—from both Hydra and the Wrecking Crew—the Avengers found that when they worked together, they could beat any foe.

There came a day when the original Avengers fought side by side with the new Avengers. And on that day it no longer mattered who was an original Avenger and who was a new recruit. From then on . . .

... they were *all* simply Avengers.

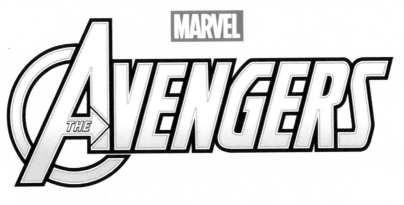

Freaky Thor Day

One morning, as the children of Hawking Elementary arrived at school, they heard a commotion on the street behind them. Thor and the Avengers had Loki cornered by the bus stop! Thor flung his mighty hammer, Mjolnir, at Loki. But Loki pulled a small glowing object covered in Asgardian runes from his pocket. He smiled deviously. Suddenly, there was a loud *BANG*, and red rays shot from the object in all directions. One of the beams glanced off Thor's hammer and headed for a group of children on the stairs!

One of the fifth graders, Kendra, was a student monitor for the kindergartners. As she stood with her group of children at the school steps, she saw Loki's energy blast coming toward them. Kendra quickly lifted her backpack to block the beam and shield the younger kids. The blast hit her bag with a loud *POP!* Everyone was safe—but when the smoke cleared, Loki was gone!

Right away, Kendra felt a change in her backpack—it was heavy and seemed to pulse with energy. But before she could examine it more closely, the teachers hustled all the children into the school. Kendra craned her neck to catch one last glimpse of Thor, her favorite Avenger, before the doors shut behind her.

Outside, Thor knew something was wrong. He grasped the handle of his hammer, Mjolnir, and spun it around. Nothing happened. Thor could lift Mjolnir, but it seemed to be an ordinary, powerless hammer.

"What is it?" Iron Man asked Thor.

"Something's wrong. Though I still have my Asgardian powers, I think . . . Mjolnir's powers are gone."

Kendra headed to science lab. She was pretty sure the most exciting part of her day had already passed—probably the most exciting part of her entire life, too. Nothing would top seeing Thor in action! As Kendra walked into the lab, she adjusted her backpack, which still felt extra heavy. Suddenly, she heard shouting from the back of the room.

"Ian, if you add any more of that compound, the whole thing will blow!" Kendra's friend Omar was arguing with his lab partner, Ian. Kendra ran over to their table. Ian was holding a vial of swirling red liquid over the bubbling beaker of their experiment. Just as Kendra reached them, Ian tilted his hand and began to pour the contents of the vial into the beaker.

Everything went into slow motion. Kendra saw the first drop hit the hot liquid, then an explosion that practically froze in time. Fragments of glass and boiling-hot chemicals hung in midair as they sprayed toward her classmates. Kendra's backpack seemed to pulse with energy.

She wasn't sure what made her do it, but she pulled off her backpack and began to spin it up and around in giant circles—the way she'd seen Thor swing Mjolnir that morning. The green-and-blue bag spun perfectly, swirling around and around to create a powerful vortex that sucked up the explosion, neutralizing it.

Time snapped back into normal speed. No one was hurt. When Kendra looked down, her backpack was in her hand again. Had she imagined the whole thing? She looked around. Only one person seemed to have noticed what really happened—the new substitute science teacher, Ms. Castro. She looked at Kendra curiously, then pulled out a phone with an odd symbol of an eagle on it and made a call.

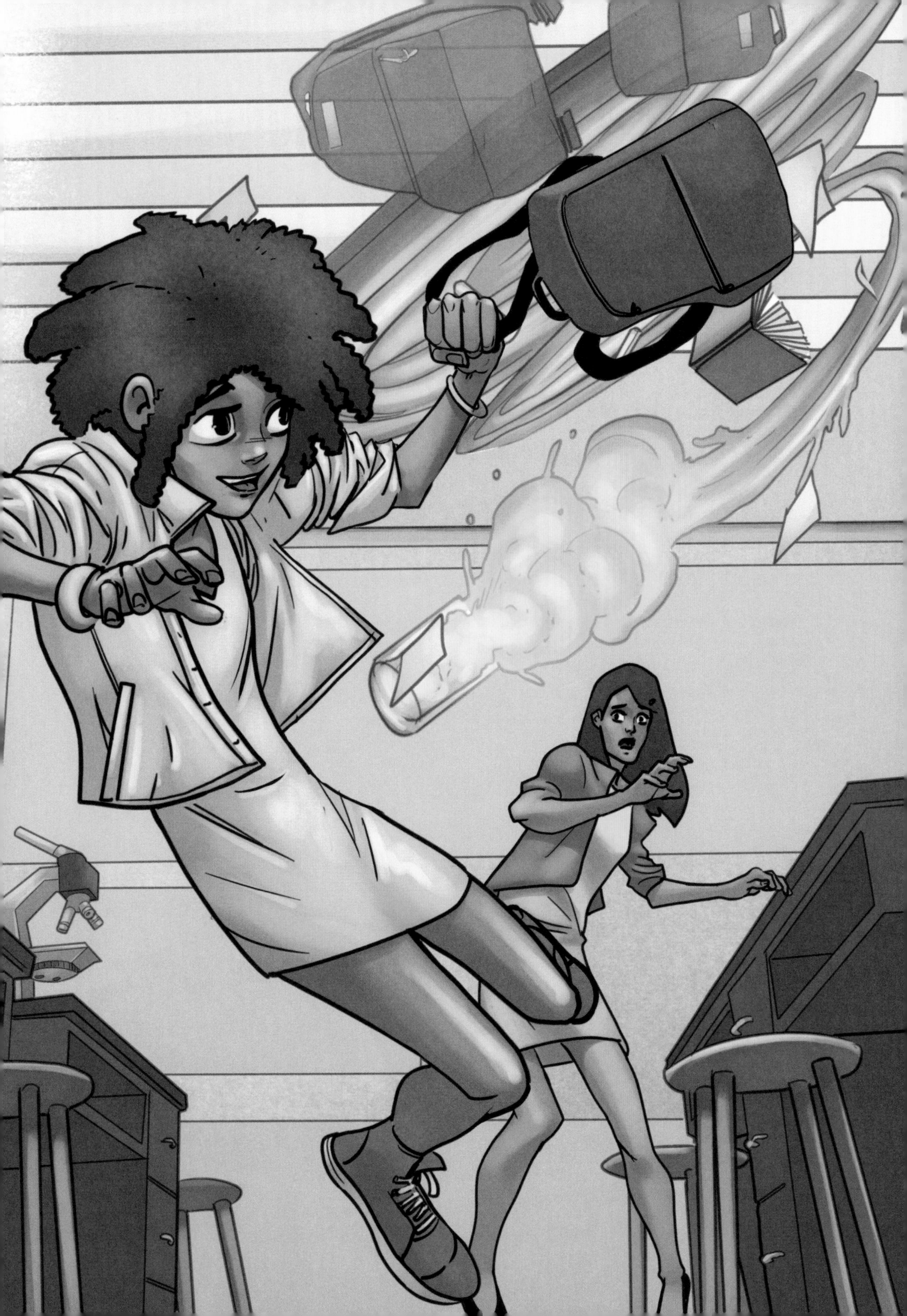

At S.H.I.E.L.D. headquarters, Thor and Nick Fury pored over a surveillance video of that morning's encounter.

"There—right there." Thor tapped on the screen.

"Looks like Loki's mystical blast glanced off Mjolnir," said Fury.

"That must have stripped away the powers of my hammer," Thor said. "But where did they go?"

"Let's find out." Fury tapped the screen again, and they watched the video play in ultra-slow motion. Just then, Ms. Castro's face popped up on the communication screen.

"Agent Castro?"

"Fury," Ms. Castro said in a low voice, "it's a good thing you stationed me at the school to monitor for aftereffects of the Avengers' battle with Loki. You and Thor should come back to Hawking Elementary right away. Something odd is happening. . . ."

On her way to recess, Kendra tried to figure out what was going on with her backpack. She took a peek inside, but she didn't see anything odd or out of place.

Something must have happened when it was hit with that blast, she thought. *But what?*

She spotted Omar on the playground. He was being hassled by Ian and his cronies. A group of kids had gathered around them. Kendra jumped up and down to see over their heads.

"Awww, Omar's little girlfriend is here to save him," Ian sneered.

"Just shut it, Ian," Omar shouted.

"What did you say?"

"I said *shut it!*"

Ian pulled back his fist to punch Omar. Kendra was too far away to stop him, but she had an idea. She held her backpack high in the air, the way Thor held his hammer. She felt energy crackling around her. Suddenly, lightning flashed and a powerful clap of thunder shook the air around them—*KRA-KOOOOM!*

Ian and the other kids gasped and ran toward the school doors.

"How did you do that?" Omar asked Kendra.

Kendra shook her head in wonder. "Maybe—" she started to say. But then she saw Ms. Castro hurrying toward them. "Sorry, Omar. I've gotta go." Kendra ran from the playground.

Thor and Nick Fury arrived at the school moments later. Ms. Castro met them at the door.

"Kendra's gone," she said.

"Where?" Fury asked.

"I don't know."

"Agent Castro, did she have a backpack with her?" Thor asked.

"Yes. She's done some rather *interesting* things with it today," Agent Castro said. "Do you know something about that?"

Fury and Thor looked at each other.

Thor took a deep breath before he spoke. "Loki's blast gave Kendra's bag the powers of Mjolnir."

Kendra wondered whether she was dreaming—her day was getting weirder by the minute. She had to find Thor and figure out why her backpack seemed to have the same abilities as his hammer. But as she turned the corner by the bank, she heard an alarm and yelling from inside. Three masked men burst out the bank doors and headed right for her.

Kendra wanted to run, but she knew what she had to do. She slid her backpack off her shoulder and threw it in the air. It flew as straight as an arrow toward the bank robbers and knocked them down like bowling pins: one, two, three! Instinctively, she reached out her arm, and the bag returned to her hand.

"Getting pretty good with that, Kendra," said someone with a deep voice behind her.

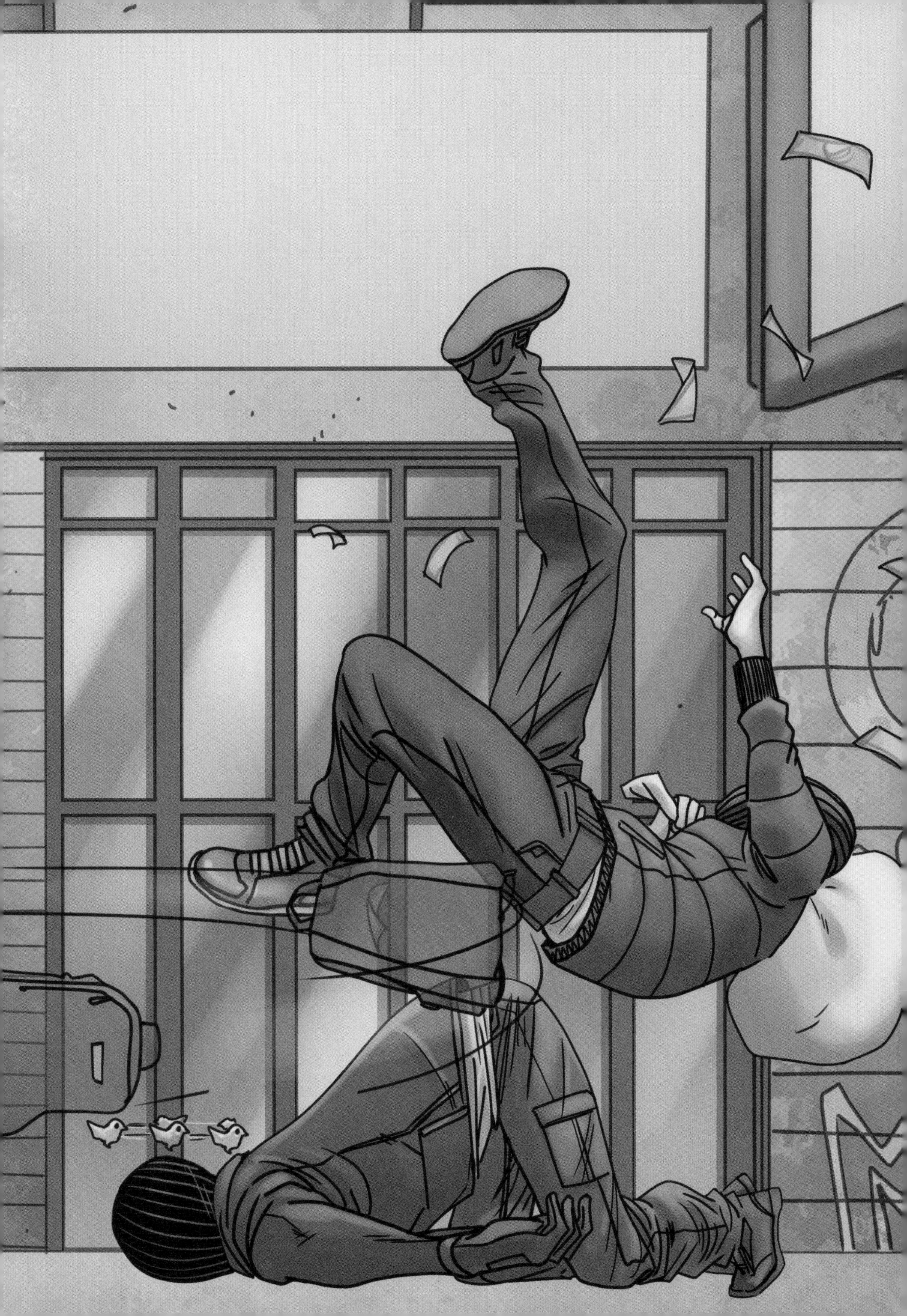

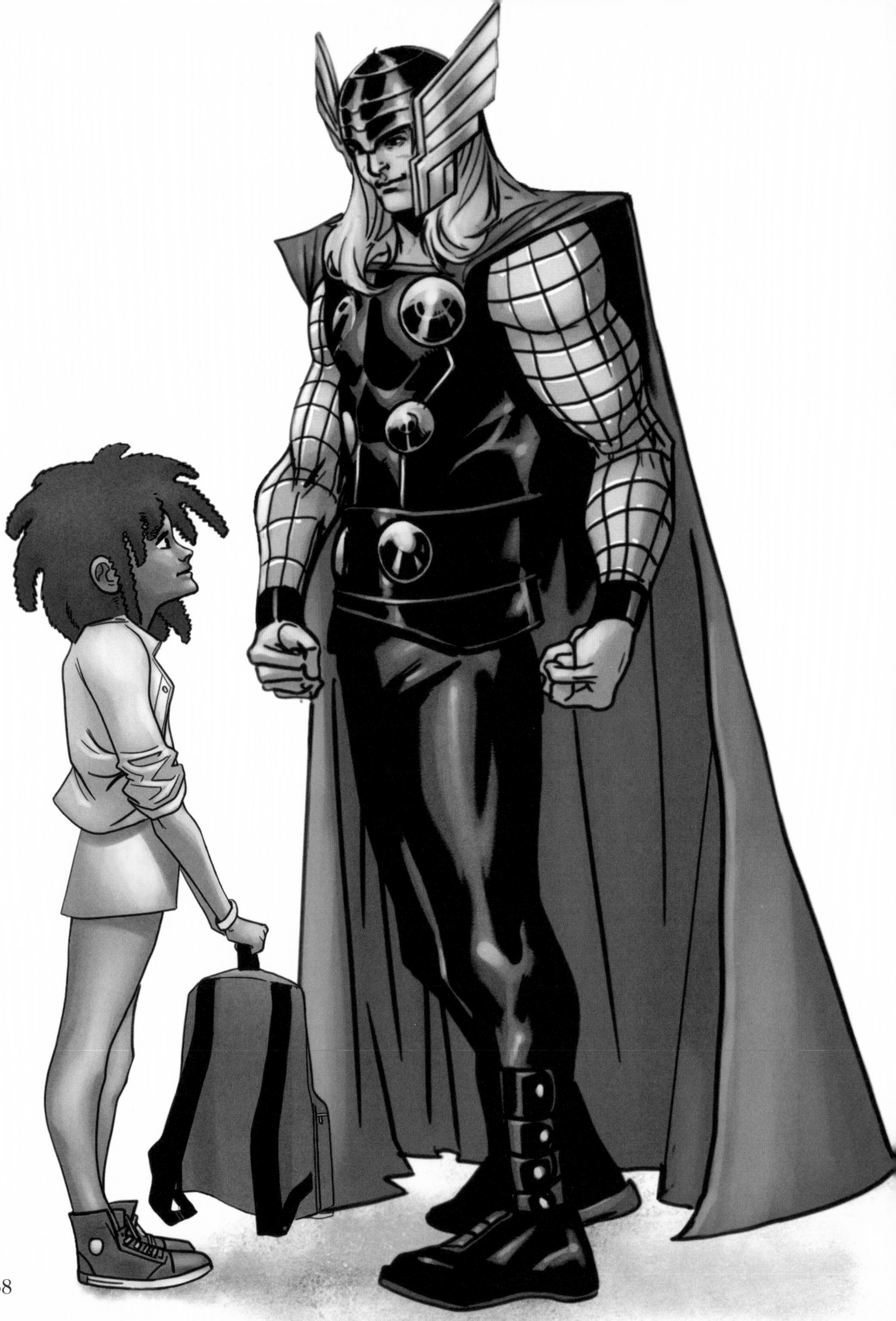

Kendra turned slowly.

"Thor!"

"You've protected a lot of people today," he said. "How are you feeling?"

"Pretty tired, actually," Kendra said.

"That kind of power can be a lot to manage," Thor said gravely.

"Especially without practice," added Nick Fury. "Though for someone with no formal training . . ." He trailed off, lost in thought.

Thor smiled at Kendra. "But you proved you have a brave and worthy heart, Kendra. Especially when you selflessly protected those children from Loki's blast this morning. That's why you could bear Mjolnir's weight and wield its power. But now we need to get your bag to S.H.I.E.L.D. labs to reverse the power transfer."

Kendra nodded and handed the bag to him.

"We'll have this back to you soon," he promised.

They began to walk away. But then Fury suddenly stopped and turned back to Kendra. "Have you considered a career in fighting global threats against hum—?"

"Fury," Thor interrupted. "That can wait. We have to go now."

The next morning, Kendra's backpack was waiting for her in the front hall. She picked it up—it felt normal again. She tried spinning and throwing it, but it just landed with a pleasant thud a few feet away. When Kendra opened the backpack, she smiled. Inside the front pocket was a note.

At that moment, Kendra decided maybe that had been the most exciting day of her whole life.

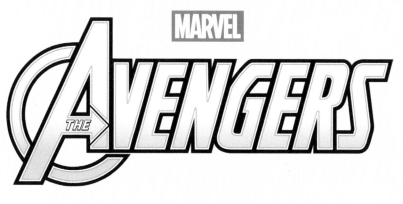

Robin Hawk

Clint Barton loved being Hawkeye. But sometimes he didn't feel as confident as his fellow Avenger Tony Stark. Tony had awesome armor, and he was a genius. As the billionaire inventor unveiled his new experimental time machine, Hawkeye thought, *Tony is always so cool, funny, and relaxed. Even when he's making a cheesy speech about time travel.*

But the demonstration was interrupted by M.O.D.O.K.! The calculating criminal glided into view, firing energy beams from his gleaming hover chair. “Look at all this nice and shiny Stark Industries technology,” he cackled. “It’s just what I need to help me conquer the world!” As Tony raced to don his Iron Man armor, Hawkeye slid forward and fired an arrow that encased M.O.D.O.K. in a cloud of smoke, confusing him.

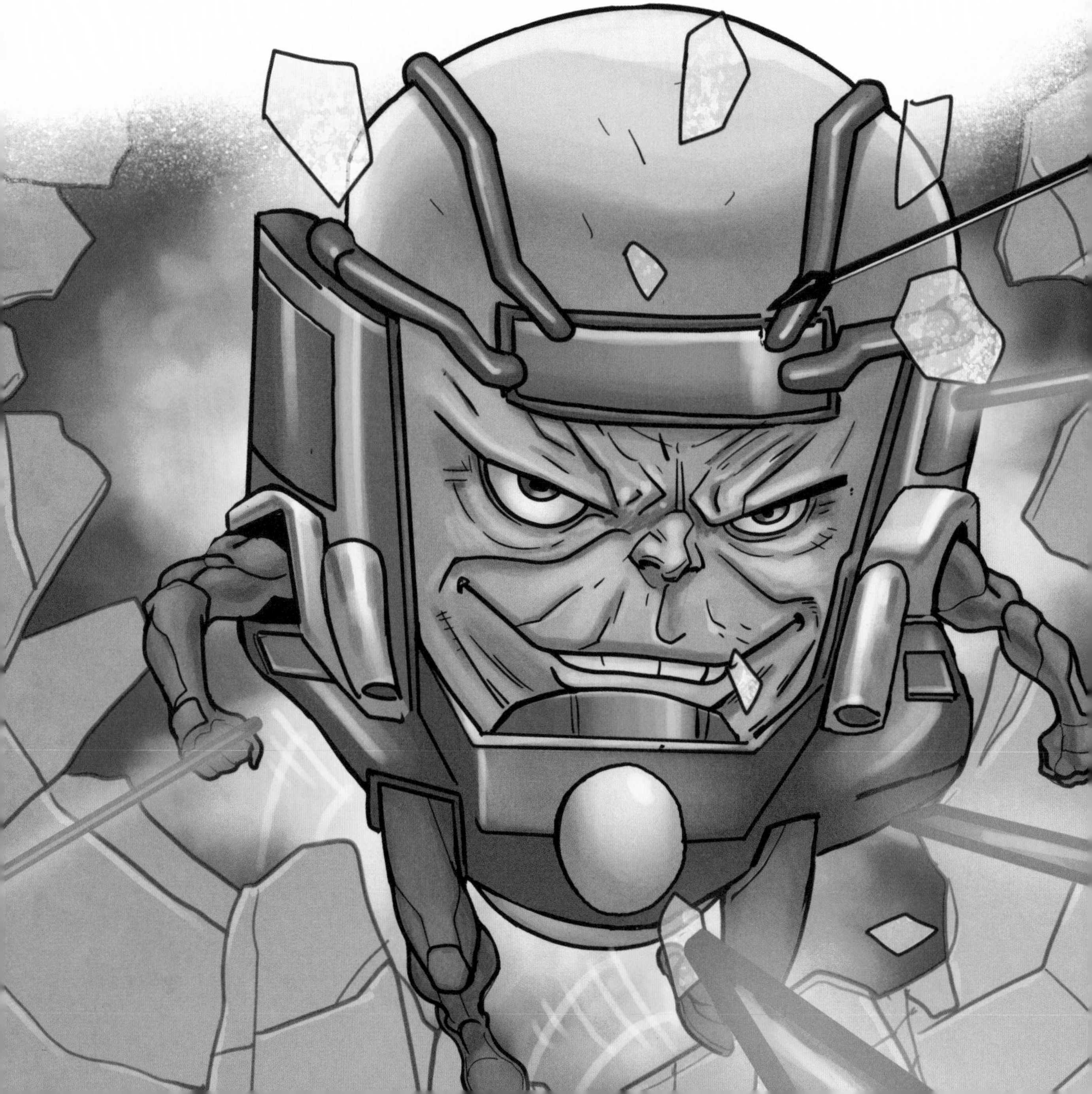

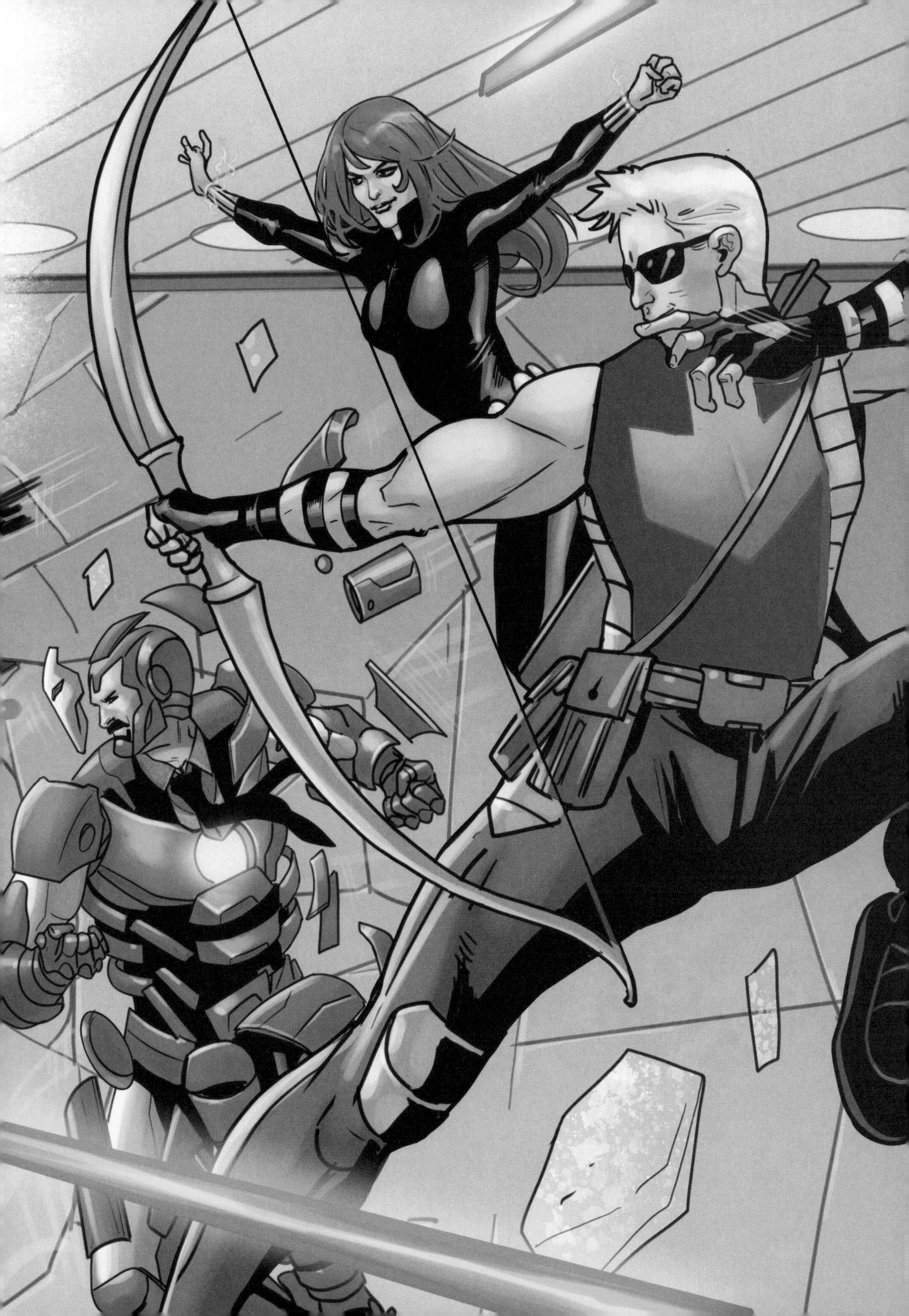

In his baffled state, the floating Super Villain accidentally knocked both himself and Iron Man toward the time machine's glowing energy field. Hawkeye jumped forward to yank Iron Man away from the machine—but he was pulled into its energy field, too! All three disappeared, along with the time machine itself.

The trio *reappeared* in a field, surrounded by bleachers full of people. *Maybe we're at a ball game,* thought Hawkeye. Then he noticed that everyone in the bleachers was dressed strangely. No cell phones, sunglasses, or baseball caps. On a faraway hill, Hawkeye saw a castle. It looked like something out of a fairy tale. Clint pulled Tony close and whispered, "I think we're in the Middle Ages!"

Just then, a squire approached Iron Man and asked, "Are you here for the jousting tournament, sir knight?" The armored Avenger removed his helmet, waved at the crowd, and flashed them a charming grin. They applauded wildly.

Hawkeye couldn't believe it. *Wow,* he thought. *Even in the Middle Ages, Tony's the coolest person here!*

Suddenly, the people in the bleachers pointed behind Clint and yelled, "Ogre! Ogre!" Hawkeye spun around to see M.O.D.O.K. sneaking away with the time machine in his clutches. Tony flew over and snatched back the device. That enraged the brainy bad guy, who attacked Tony with an energy blast. Reeling from the impact, Iron Man aimed his repulsors at M.O.D.O.K., but all that came out was a bit of black smoke. The time machine's energy field had shorted out Tony's repulsor beams!

Thinking fast, Hawkeye shot a trio of explosive arrows at M.O.D.O.K. The blasts damaged the Super Villain's hover chair, but he escaped into the nearby forest, roaring, "This isn't over, archer!"

The townspeople crowded around Hawkeye, proclaiming, "It's *him*! It's the legendary Robin Hood!"

Hawkeye shook his head, shouting, "No, you've got it all wrong! I'm *not* Robin Hood!"

The villagers cheered, "Only Robin Hood would be so modest!" They thanked Hawkeye for saving them from the "ogre," and they marveled at his archery skills. Now Clint knew what it was like to be cool. The local blacksmith even presented him with a *special* arrow.

But then the town crier approached Hawkeye, pleading, "The ogre is rampaging through the forest! Won't you come help us, brave Robin Hood?"

Hawkeye answered, "Of course!" But he felt bad. Nobody deserved to be called an ogre, not even M.O.D.O.K. So Clint added, "He's not *actually* an ogre. You see, he's a biomechanical living computer. . . ." The town crier just stared at him blankly. It was too difficult to explain. "Um, let's go get the ogre," Clint said with a sigh, then followed the town crier with Tony.

Hawkeye and Iron Man knew that M.O.D.O.K. was too dangerous to be left to roam free in the Middle Ages. They had to capture the floating felon and get back home!

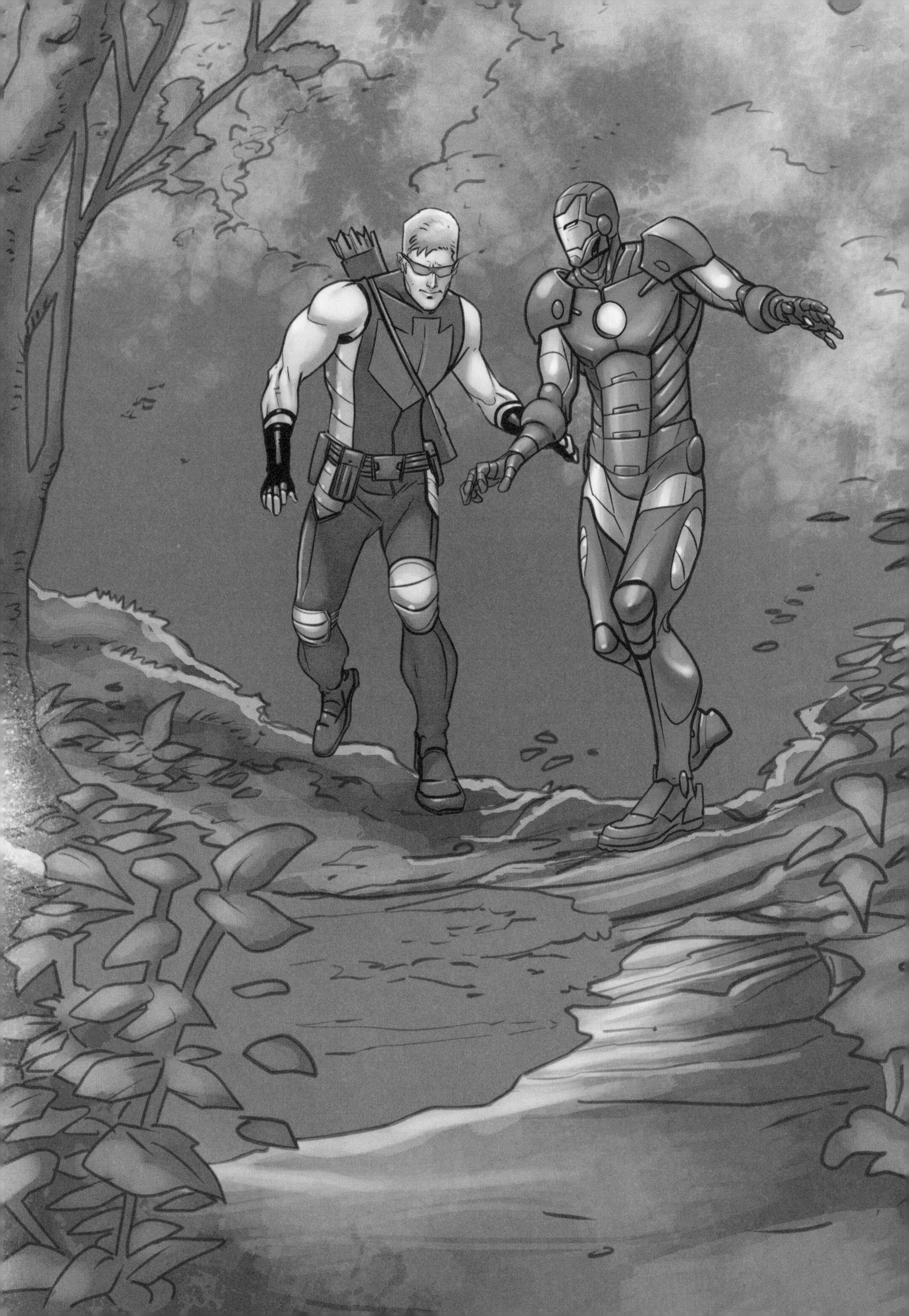

Hawkeye and Iron Man crept into the forest, where M.O.D.O.K. was hiding, but the clever criminal was prepared for them. Tony accidentally stepped on a trip wire. Before he knew it, he was trapped in a cage made of tree branches. But Tony had his own tricks. Using his rocket boosters, he broke free of the trap.

While M.O.D.O.K. was distracted by Iron Man, Hawkeye fired an arrow at him. The arrow covered the super-sized Super Villain in an electric net. Now that he was Hawkeye's prisoner, M.O.D.O.K. admitted that he needed the two heroes to get back to his own time. "This primitive era is not the proper place for a genius like me," he said with a sniff. *Besides*, M.O.D.O.K. thought, *after I'm back in the present, I can just snatch the time machine from these do-gooders.*

Iron Man activated the time machine. The little device hummed to life. All three time travelers stepped inside the machine's energy field and found themselves back in the present.

Iron Man and Hawkeye reeled for a moment, disoriented by the journey. M.O.D.O.K. took that opportunity to grab the time machine! But just as he was about to activate it, Hawkeye shot a grappling-hook arrow at the device. The arrow latched on to the time machine, ripping it from M.O.D.O.K.'s clutches. When M.O.D.O.K. tried to take it back, he found himself surrounded by Avengers. His hover chair, still damaged, made a sad sputtering noise.

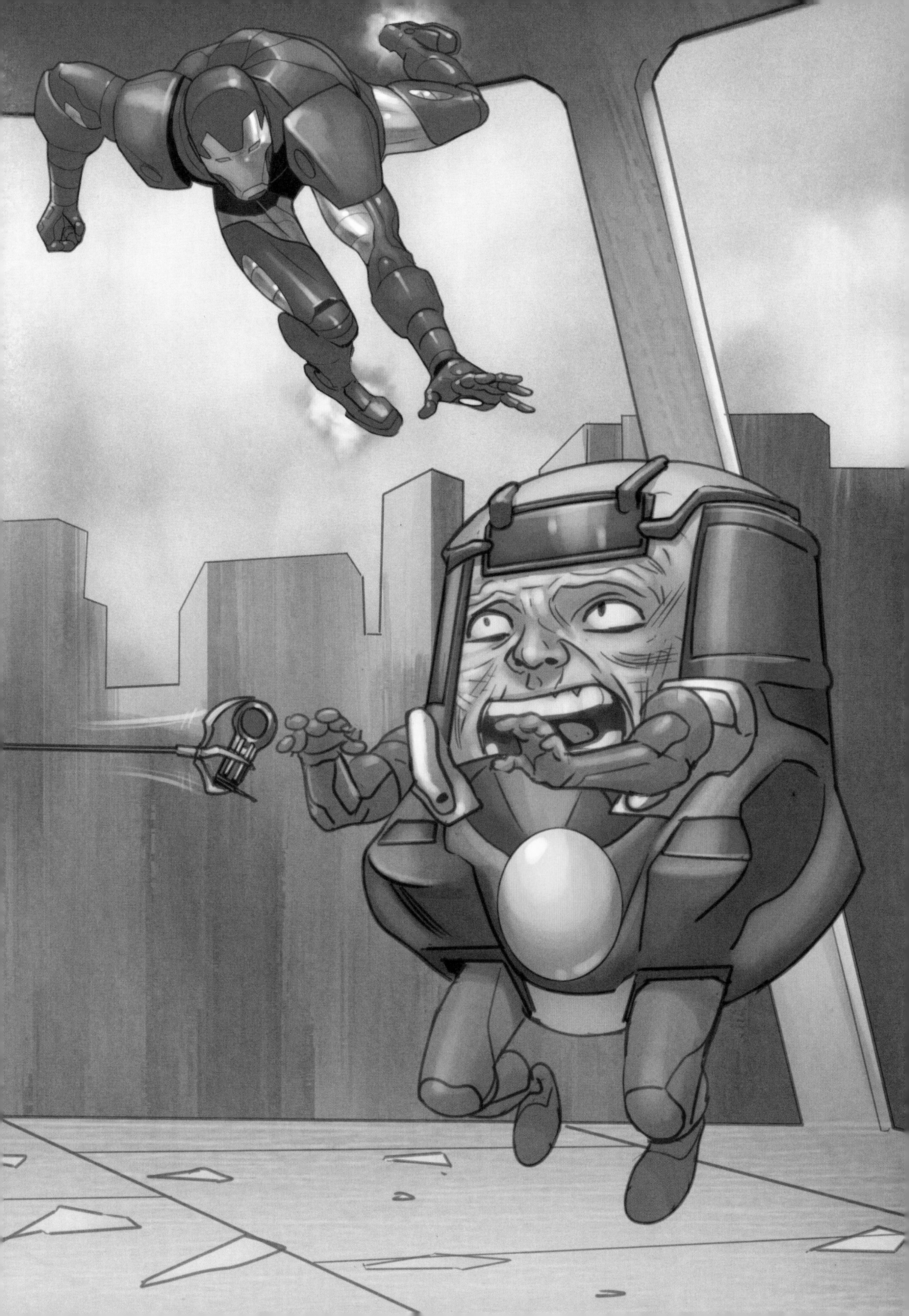

After M.O.D.O.K. had been led away by S.H.I.E.L.D. agents, Tony remarked that it had looked like Hawkeye was enjoying himself in the Middle Ages.

"Y'know, I used to think that I wasn't as cool as you," Hawkeye admitted.

"Come on," Tony said. "That's nonsense."

"Well, that's what I learned on this last adventure," Clint said with a nod. "I also learned that archery is cool in *any* time period." He grinned.

With that, he pulled out a souvenir he'd brought home from their trip. It was the arrow the village blacksmith had given him. And as Tony examined it closely, he saw that it was decorated with a painting of Hawkeye . . . *dressed as Robin Hood*!

"Does that make you Robin Hawk, then?" Tony asked. The two Super Heroes shared a laugh.

Later that night, Tony decided to do a little research. When he looked for Robin Hood on the Internet, Tony almost fell out of his chair. On his computer screen, there were many drawings of Robin Hood, but they all had one thing in common: Robin Hood always wore a purple arrow on his chest, just like Hawkeye's!

Friends for Life

The Avengers were on the scene of a bank robbery by the Super Villain called the Absorbing Man! But Captain America and Iron Man were needed for another mission, so Vision—the Avengers' newest member—jumped into action!

The Absorbing Man can turn into any substance he touches—such as metal or concrete. And if that isn't bad enough, he also carries a ball and chain for extra clobbering power!

With all the excitement around the Avengers showing up, a
crowd had begun to form.

"What's this? A *junior* Avenger? I'm insulted," taunted the
Absorbing Man. He started to transform into metal as he swung
his ball and chain around, preparing to pulverize Vision!

"I can't let you hurt any of these people, Absorbing Man!"
Vision was flying so fast toward the Absorbing Man that the
crowd was sure they both would explode when they collided!

But Vision had many powers other than flight!

Surprising the crowd, the Absorbing Man's blow went right through Vision as if he were a ghost! That was how Vision got his name: he looked like a "strange vision" when he became intangible.

The Absorbing Man was shocked. "What the—?" he cried. Now that the villain was off balance and couldn't get out of the Avenger's way, Vision pulled his fist back and . . .

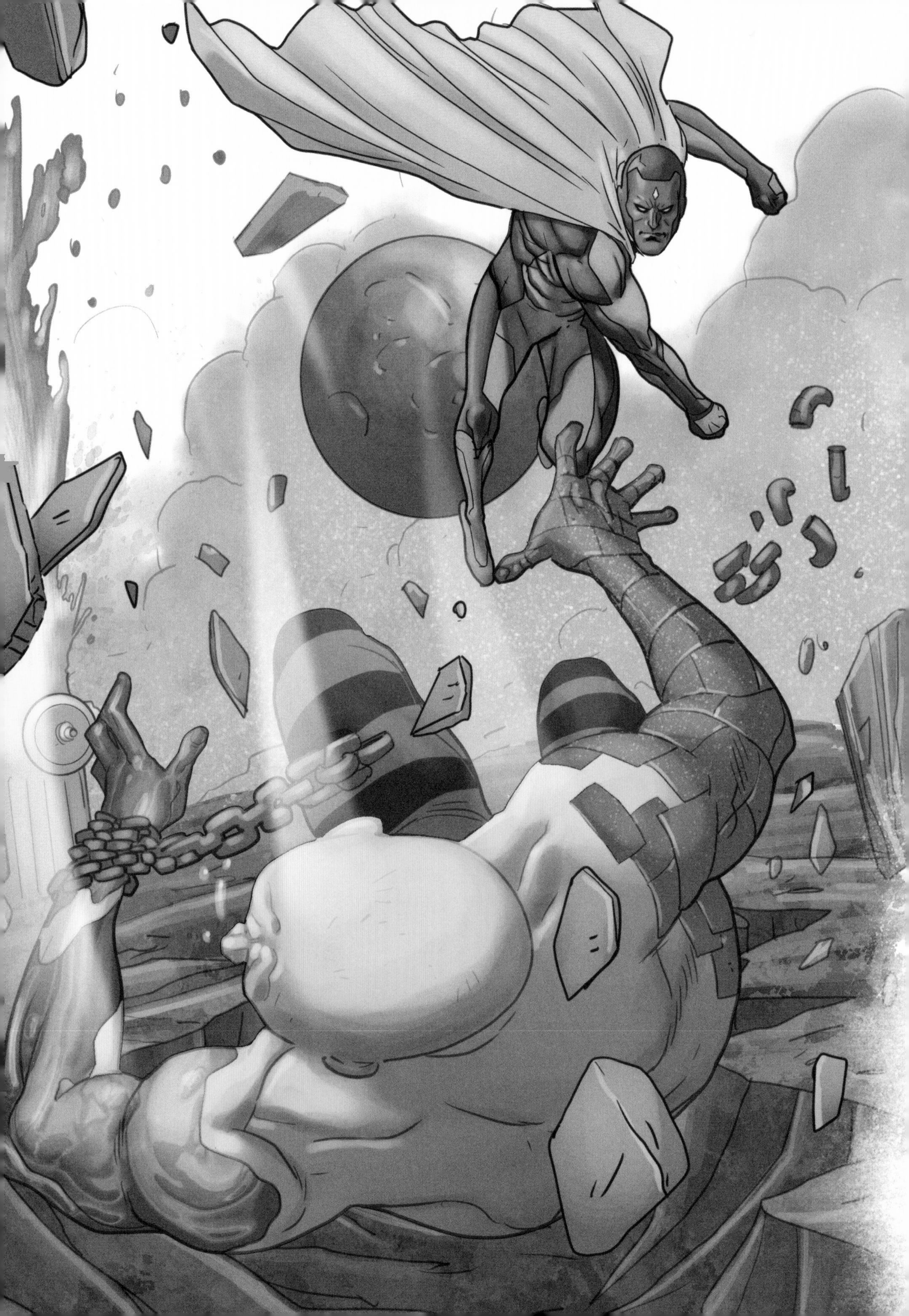

The crowd scattered with the power of Vision's punch! In
the confusion, a ten-year-old boy named Derek got separated
from his parents. He couldn't find them anywhere!

After making sure the Absorbing Man wouldn't give the
police any more trouble, Vision scanned the area and noticed
Derek frantically searching the crowd. Derek was scared already,
having lost his parents, but what really scared him . . .

. . . was Vision himself! Vision was an android. An android was a robot shaped like a person but made of plastic and metal—and Vision had a bright red face! To make matters worse, Vision didn't always understand human emotions . . . especially when they weren't based on logic. He was a little confused as to why the boy was still terrified after the Super Villain had gone. He finally asked, "May I help you?"

But Derek was still afraid, even when Vision offered to help him. "Whatever you are," Derek yelled, "stay away from me!" Sometimes androids had a hard time making friends.

Vision saw his reflection in Derek's helmet and realized androids could be scary to humans. "I am called Vision. I am here to help you," he said. "I may look like a robot, but I am still a nice person. What is your name?"

Derek was unsure of what he should do. Vision looked so stiff—so much like a machine—that Derek was nervous about talking with him. Derek stuck out his tongue at Vision just to see what the android would do. Vision was confused at first but then decided to play along!

After their short game, Derek felt better about talking with Vision. "I'm Derek," he said. "I've lost my parents, and I want to go home." Vision saw that Derek was nervous about finding his parents.

To help take Derek's mind off his worry, Vision asked, "How would you like to see some of the things I can do?"

Derek nervously asked, "Like what?"

Vision continued to scan the crowd for Derek's parents, but he didn't see them yet. He knew he needed to distract Derek until he found them. "Like this!" Vision put his hand over Derek's head, and the ends of the boy's hair jumped toward Vision's hand!

Derek laughed. "Whoa! How do you do that?"

Vision explained, "By moving my electrical currents around, I can create static electricity so that your hair stands up on your head."

"How about this?" Vision asked before he walked right through a wall. Derek was afraid for a moment that Vision had left him, but Vision popped out of the wall behind Derek and surprised him— "Gotcha!"

"That's so cool," Derek said. "You can play a lot of tricks on people with that power, I bet!"

"I like to spook Captain America whenever I get the chance," Vision said.

Derek laughed. "You play jokes on Captain America? On *the* Captain America? I can't believe it!"

"I am stronger than humans, too! But don't worry—I never use my strength against normal people, just the really bad ones," Vision said.

"This is so much fun!" Derek said. He wished he had Vision's powers!

Vision was confused. He asked, "What is fun? How do you get it?"

"You don't know what fun is?" Derek asked. "Well, I'll show you!" Derek strapped on his helmet and jumped on his skateboard to show off his moves! Vision watched Derek and wondered whether he could skateboard, too.

It turned out that androids were not built to skateboard. But even though Vision wasn't good at skateboarding, he started to feel something he had never felt before.

Derek pointed at Vision with glee. "Is that a smile?" asked Derek. "Yes, I think it is! Vision, you're having fun!"

Now that Derek was getting to know Vision—and had seen him smile—he started to feel safe with the android. Derek taught Vision how to have fun. Because they were learning from each other, they were becoming friends! And being friends with an Avenger was awesome!

"You really want to skateboard? Let me show you how I would do it," Vision said with a grin.

"Sounds like fun!" Derek smiled back.

Vision flew, with Derek riding him like a skateboard! "This is how Avengers have fun, Derek!"

Derek was so excited he yelled out, *"Wahoo!"*

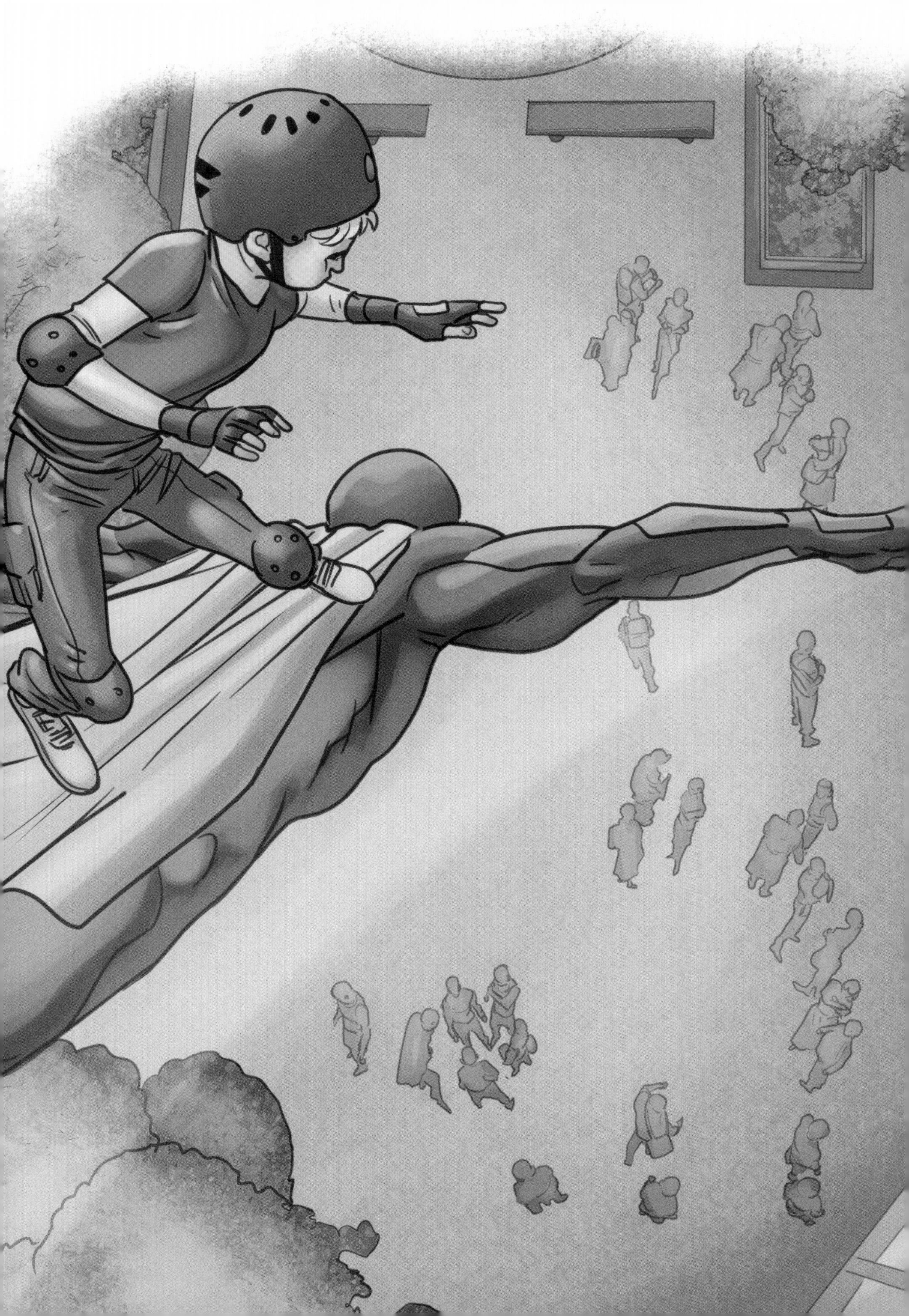

Derek's parents heard the shout and knew it was their son! They yelled to Derek as they ran across the street toward him and Vision. Vision, alarmed by the yells, thought Derek might be in danger and stood in front of him protectively.

But then Vision saw the love on their faces and noticed that they had the same eye and hair colors as Derek. Derek's parents were found! "Mom! Dad!" Derek yelled. Their family was back together.

Vision knew that Derek would no longer want to spend time with him now that he had found his parents. That made Vision feel sad, another emotion he had not experienced before!

Derek's parents were glad Vision had taken care
of their son. But they were worried because danger often
surrounded the Avengers. "Thank you for taking care of
Derek, Vision," Derek's dad said. "Don't take this the wrong
way, but is he really safe with you? What if you get attacked
by a Super Villain while Derek is with you?"

Vision—feeling even sadder and realizing that perhaps
Derek's father was correct—began to float up and away
to return to his lonely life. "I would never let anyone or
anything harm Derek. His safety is my first priority."

"Don't be mean, Dad! There's nothing to be afraid of,"
Derek said. "Vision is an Avenger and a hero. But most of all . . .

". . . Vision is my friend!" Just hearing Derek call him a friend made Vision feel good inside. He had never had a real friend before, aside from the Avengers. Derek's father relaxed and thanked Vision for keeping Derek safe.

Derek's father shook Vision's hand and asked, "Would you like to come to dinner with us, Vision? Seems the least we can do after you found Derek."

Vision cracked a big smile. "I have other matters I need to attend to, sir. But perhaps I could visit Derek tomorrow. We could go to the park together. I need to practice my skateboarding!"

Vision learned about friendship that day and how to have fun! Derek made a new friend and learned that just because something was different did not mean he should be afraid of it.

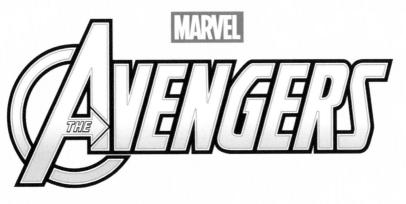

The Rise of a New Team

Just as the newest Avengers were finishing their training exercises, they received a call from Nick Fury.

"Looks like the old-timers need some help," Fury said. S.H.I.E.L.D. had sent the Avengers to investigate a secret Hydra base, but they had all mysteriously disappeared at once!

"It's not like the Avengers to be missing in action," Falcon said. They headed out to look for their friends.

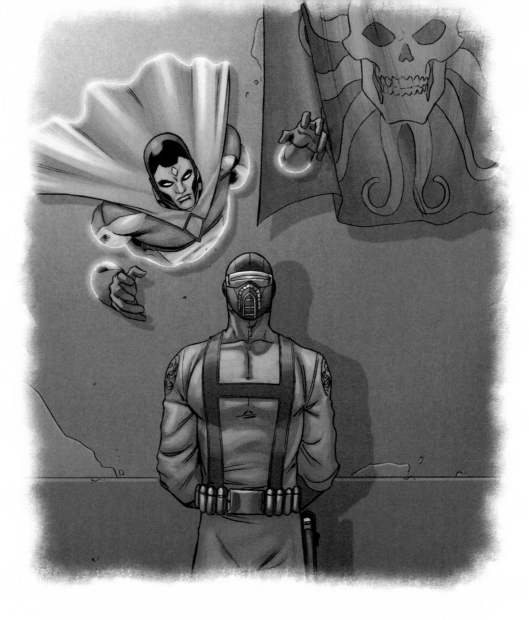

When they arrived at the hidden Hydra base, the Avengers
decided to take the enemy by surprise. Vision used his powers
to float effortlessly through the wall. He appeared behind
a Hydra guard. Vision tapped on the unsuspecting guard's
left shoulder and then disappeared behind the wall again.
Confused, the agent turned around and saw nothing. But then
he felt a tap on his right shoulder. That time, he was startled
to see Vision grinning back at him! Vision didn't stay friendly
for long. Within seconds, he had taken out the agent.

Just then, the rest of the Avengers joined the attack! Quicksilver dashed in before anyone could spot him.

"Hi, there! Nice to meet you!" Quicksilver greeted his victims with a handshake before he knocked them out. Soon he was deep inside the base.

Quicksilver's twin sister, Scarlet Witch, was someone else who should not be messed with. She used her magic to stop the Hydra agents from grabbing their weapons.

"Wait a minute, boys," Scarlet Witch said.

By then, Hydra knew it was under attack. Vision, Quicksilver, and Scarlet Witch were surrounded and outnumbered. Suddenly, Falcon shot through the air and swooped in on them! With a mighty cry, he blasted his fléchettes!

Meanwhile, time was running out for Hawkeye and Black Widow. Falcon, Quicksilver, and Scarlet Witch were only distracting Hydra so Hawkeye and Black Widow could slip in unnoticed. They had to find their friends! Hawkeye made sure to create a clear path for Black Widow by taking out any villains in their way.

The coast was clear, and soon Black Widow was near the computer with the confidential files that would reveal the other Avengers' location.

Quickly and carefully, she decoded the password and unlocked the files. But they'd been spotted! A huge Hydra agent charged toward Black Widow. He was twice her size! Hawkeye was already fighting off Hydra agents by the door. Luckily, Black Widow was the type of person who could handle challenges herself . . . no matter how difficult. With a swift high kick, Black Widow put the agent on the ground—and she knew exactly where the Avengers were!

Though the Avengers had taken on an entire Hydra base, they were in for even bigger trouble. Their friends were locked in Ultron's hidden lab! All along, Hydra had been helping Ultron take down the Avengers. Ultron planned to brainwash the Avengers into working for him.

It was a good thing the new team of Avengers had assembled!

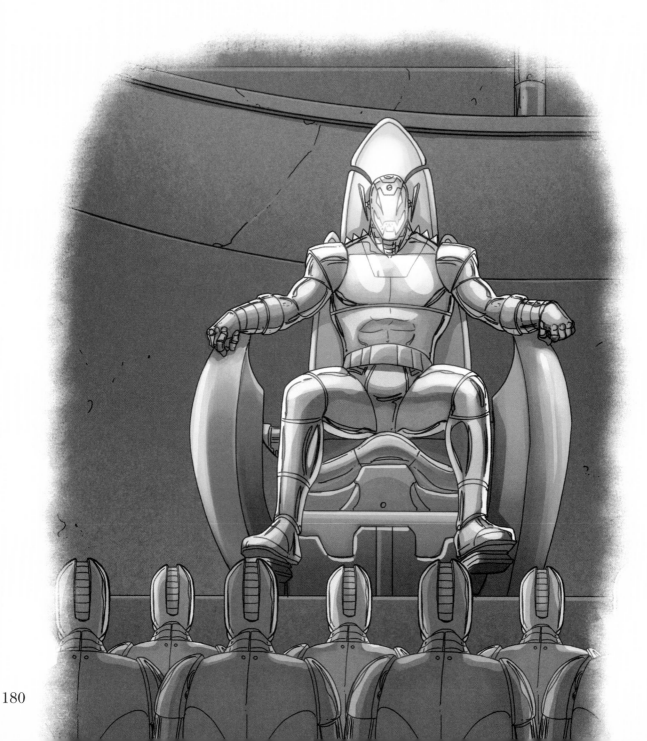

Black Widow discovered that Ultron was hiding deep underground. He had built an army of Subultrons—miniature versions of himself—so no one could get to him or his captives.

"I have a plan! We have to act fast, but it just might work," Black Widow said.

"Well, it's a good thing I'm here," said Quicksilver, smirking.

Black Widow and Hawkeye took the lead and snuck into Ultron's hideout. Together, they took down the guards on the ground.

Falcon waited patiently for the signal from the super spies. Finally, it was time! Just before Black Widow and Hawkeye approached the troop of Subultrons, Falcon jumped in! He opened his wings and dove right into the thick of their ranks from behind. The Subultrons didn't even hear Falcon coming until he had fired his fléchettes!

Finally, the Avengers surrounded the sinister Ultron.

"You believe I cannot defeat all six of you? I crushed the original Avengers. It won't take too long to crush the new recruits." Ultron laughed.

"Don't be so sure of yourself," Scarlet Witch said through gritted teeth.

"The next time you see your friends, they will be working for me!" Ultron roared.

With everything they had, the Avengers charged at Ultron!

Quicksilver ducked away from the fighting. He had to act fast, before Ultron realized what was happening. Earlier, Scarlet Witch had used her powers to find out where Ultron had locked up their friends. Quicksilver raced to free them.

"Are you guys okay?" Quicksilver asked.

"Yes, pull that lever over there! It will turn off the electrical-wave seat belt, but an alarm will sound," Cap shouted.

"The rest are taking care of that metal maniac right now," Quicksilver replied.

On the other side of the building, Ultron heard the alarm go off. Soon Cap, Thor, Hulk, and Quicksilver joined the fight. Ultron looked around. His entire army of Subultrons had been destroyed. He was the only one left. He could barely handle six Avengers, and now the entire team was ready for battle. Ultron knew he would lose that fight. There was only one thing left to do—he blasted a hole to his secret getaway.

"This will not be the last time we meet," he snarled before disappearing.

Though Ultron had escaped, all the Avengers were happy everyone was safe and reunited again. Nick Fury was glad to have everyone back together. "You see what teamwork can do?" he told the Avengers.

But the Avengers all knew how important it was to work together and help one another when help was needed. After all, they were a team: the new team of Avengers. But there was no team without Iron Man!

"Where's Iron Man?" Vision asked as they started to head back to the S.H.I.E.L.D. Helicarrier.

"We thought he was with you," Thor said as he glanced around.

"No, we thought he was with you and Ultron . . ." Hawkeye said, shaking his head.

Where could the invincible Iron Man be?